A LENAPE LEGACY

DORIS WILBUR

Travel with Amelia into the woods and into the life of some Native Americans ...

DORIS WILBUR

MILFORD HOUSE

an imprint of Sunbury Press, Inc.
Mechanicsburg, PA USA

MILFORD HOUSE

an imprint of Sunbury Press, Inc.
Mechanicsburg, PA USA

For information about special discounts for bulk purchases, please contact Sunbury Press Orders Dept. at (855) 338-8359 or orders@sunburypress.com.

To request one of our authors for speaking engagements or book signings, please contact Sunbury Press Publicity Dept. at publicity@sunburypress.com.

ISBN: 978-1-62006-061-2 (Trade paperback)

Library of Congress Control Number: 2018952283

FIRST MILFORD HOUSE PRESS EDITION: July 2018

Product of the United States of America
0 1 1 2 3 5 8 13 21 34 55

Set in Bookman Old Style
Designed by Crystal Devine
Cover by Terry Kennedy
Cover art by Doris Wilbur
Edited by Erika Hodges

Continue the Enlightenment!

PROLOGUE

EFORE THE SIGNING OF THE DECLARATION of Independence, many foreign countries were scrambling to gain control of the wild lands in the northeastern part of America. Newly formed territories had vague, undulating boundary lines that changed often. France, the Netherlands, and Britain were all eager to broaden their holdings and add to their possessions. Fearful that the French and Dutch entrepreneurs would move in and claim much of the New World land, the British authorities urged all colonial settlers to move further into the interior from their coastal and river settlements. It was important to get Britain's rights to that soil firmly established. Land agents made generous offers to anyone wanting to homestead to purchase land for very low prices, or free, just by staking out property and putting up a dwelling.

Many young couples near the growing port cities in Pennsylvania and Virginia lived as sharecroppers and worked the land for wealthy Englishmen. These landowners had come to America and bought up large parcels of land or they were privileged gentry who had been given hundreds of acres by the King of England. Despite working from dawn to dark, everything the sharecroppers earned somehow went right back into the landholder's fat pockets. Sharecroppers were breaking their backs just to subsist and had nothing to call their own. By striking out into the wilderness and staking their claim to new land, they had a chance to build a cabin home no one could take from them. Hundreds of young, naive couples like Ina and Cornelius Benjamin seized the opportunity to make their own rules and own property to raise their family on. Despite the challenge of hardship and isolation ahead of them, Ina and Cornelius left their relatives, friends, and everything familiar to them to follow their dream. They also left all the conveniences of living in the town of Harris Landing. Unsuspecting and unschooled, they headed north into the wilds of Pennsylvania and the opportunity for adventure and prosperity it offered.

CHAPTER 1

Early Fall 1765 on the Pennsylvania Frontier

THE OUTSTRETCHED LIMBS OF THE HICKORY trees held out handfuls of green husk covered nuts on each branch. It was a plentiful harvest this year. The older folks always said it was a sure sign of a long, tough winter ahead. "Watch them apples and nuts. If they be heavy, be sure the snow will be too," they'd say.

The tall hardwood trees had grown generous crops of the large round nuts, which fell to the ground with a thud and a bounce every time the wind blew and rustled the treetops. Nuts were lying scattered like a child's game of giant, oversized marbles all around the base of the rough-barked trees.

It was a warm, fall day, blessed with golden sunshine and wisps of clouds drifting slowly on a pure cerulean blue sky. Ina Benjamin had left her cabin for the afternoon and was in the woods nearby with two of her children, Rubin and Amelia. They were picking up all they could of the fallen nuts and stuffing them into coarse muslin sacks. The shagbark hickory trees were easy to spot among the other trees in the pine and hardwood forest. Their dark, ragged bark looked like layered, rough wood shingles that were curling at the bottom edge and peeling upwards off the trunk of the large stately trees.

"The squirrels hev ben' busy here," Ina said to the children as she picked through the litter of gnawed green husks and chewed shell pieces. "They've got most of these; let's go find us another

1

tree." Her middle child, Rubin, a thin little boy of five, was delicate and too small for his age. He had wild, extra curly blonde hair that never seemed to have a part in it, although Ina put one there every morning when she combed it. She had tried to tame his unruly hair, but it quickly rearranged itself into a tumble of haphazard ringlets again. Ina didn't know why he was born with such unusual blonde hair. She and her husband Cornelius both had ordinary dark, straight hair. His aunt Marion did have hair that was sort of blonde though; maybe he got it from her side of the family. Regardless, Rubin was a beautiful, pleasant child and she loved him and her other two children dearly.

Rubin wore brown, baggy pants held up by a rope belt that was passed through the pant loops at his waist and then tied in a knot. Ina had sewn his long sleeved, light blue shirt herself, making all the small, perfect stitches by hand. He looked even frailer in his oversized clothes. They were made purposely big on him so they would last awhile. His sturdy leather shoes were too large also. They always got them made that way for the children, whose feet size changed every few months. It was hard to get anything out there in the wilds of Pennsylvania, especially luxuries like fitted shoes. The children had to stuff soft flannel cloth or wool in the toes of their big shoes when they first got them, and then take it back out when their feet grew longer. Items like shoes and cloth were sent to them from relatives back in Harris Landing and delivered whenever a trapper or hunters were passing through. If they were lucky, they got a package of clothes and other goods twice a year from relatives.

Ina's daughter Amelia, unlike frail Rubin, was a rugged child. She was eight years old and quite a tomboy. Her long brown hair was dark and straight just like her parents. She could be counted on to do whatever chores needed to be done without complaining, but she was often a dreamer and wanderer. She always took time to look for songbirds in the treetops and point them out to the others. She would stop to look at wildflowers growing along the way and see what they smelled like too. Mushrooms and moss also had to be examined, and if she came across an orange salamander she had to hold it for a while before sending it on its way. Often she just stood still, studying some crawling, hopping, or flying insect whenever one caught her eye.

Ina kept Amelia's long hair twined into braids, and what a chore it was to comb it out straight and get it braided up again each day. How that girl got so many knots and burrs in her hair was a puzzle to her. The daily hair grooming was a tortuous chore for both of them. She often had stick-to-me seeds in her hair from running in the field and one time even a bunch of burdocks were clinging tight. Ina was tempted to cut Amelia's hair short, but that was unlady-like. Even though Amelia was a tomboy, she was still her little girl.

Amelia found some treasure now and ran with her hand out-stretched toward Ina. "Look Momma, a puff ball," and she squeezed the small brown ball with the papery husk. That sent a little cloud of brown powder billowing into the air from a crack in its skin. They watched it swirl away and dissolve like smoke. "Oh, Amelia, don't waste it, we should save it case someone has a nosebleed or some-thin'. This is a great find, thanks sweetie." Ina took the puffball from Amelia's hand and carefully dropped it into her apron pocket. "Come on children, we gotta git a move on now and find more nuts," Ina said, motioning at Rubin to join her and Amelia.

They had been in this section of the woods several times before and Ina knew right where they were. It wasn't far from the log cabin where they lived back across the field. They'd cut firewood in here, hunted for herbs, gathered delicious wild blueberries from the low bushes in July, and picked blackberries along the edge of the field. Ina felt somewhat uneasy for some reason today though, so she kept the children close to where she was working. Most times it didn't matter if Rubin and Amelia wandered off to play hide and seek or swing on the wild grapevines that hung like fat ropes from the treetops. She enjoyed hearing their laughter and whoops of joy as they swung back and forth on the vines. They never went very far out of sight, and she could easily call them back, but today she didn't let them play too far away from her. She kept them working on the hickory nut gathering with her where she could keep a close eye on them. For a brief moment that morning, she had paused because she thought she smelled smoke, but then decided the fall breeze must have brought a whiff of chimney smoke from the cabin their way.

3

She could see the shaggy bark of a big hickory tree a little deeper in the woods and decided to work her way over toward it. In some areas where the forest canopy was too thick for much sun to get in, only a few plants or bushes grew. It was easy to walk under the trees there. In other parts of the woods it was much harder to walk; the treetops were more open, sunlight streamed in, and brush and sapling trees grew everywhere. Rubin and Amelia chattered away about how good the nuts tasted as treats or in Mom's cookies. However, they'd have to do the tedious work of hitting them with a mallet to crack them and pick apart the shells for the nutmeats. Ina listened to their chatter but kept looking past where they were walking, into the recesses of the woods. She couldn't quite understand or shake the uneasiness she was feeling. She almost wished she had insisted Cornelius had forgotten about chinking the logs in the cabin and came with them today. Then she felt a little foolish at her weakness. She knew these woods, and yet, she sensed something was different today. Something seemed ominous, like the sense you get of a storm coming even though the sun is shining.

Ina and Cornelius had listened intently to stories about this uninhabited, mountainous country before they moved there. Hunters and trappers had told animated tales of giant bears that lived in dark caves and wandered the woods, and roving packs of wolves that howled at night and made you afraid to close your eyes to rest. They also told about huge, stealthy mountain lions that would stalk your children and snatch them away before you knew it. One often-repeated warning was of giant birds that could lift livestock, chickens, and even small children into the air and fly off with them. But Ina and Cornelius regarded them only as exaggerated tales told around campfires and had never actually known anyone credible who saw any of those creatures or disasters happen.

Yet the remote possibility of one of those stories being true occupied the corners of Ina's mind. Although they were quite far away, she had heard packs of wolves howling several nights already. Sometimes, in the stillness of the night, she and Cornelius would hear other loud animal sounds from creatures roaming and hunting in the darkness. They spotted black bears all the time and Cornelius had even killed one that they used for meat and fur. Who knew what lived in these unexplored dark woods with all the deep valleys, rocky cliffs full of caves, and impassible high wooded peaks that descended straight up from valley floors? Anything could hide there and not be found for a long time in the dense forest of thick eastern white pine, massive maples, oaks, beech, and nut trees.

There were also tall tangles of laurel thickets that grew into mazes of limbs and leaves looming higher than a person's head. There must be hundreds of places where no man had even set a foot or eyes on yet, she thought. They weren't that far from the Indian country either, although they had been assured all the savages had been chased from this area some time ago. A loud rustle of leaves off to the right made Ina jump and she shouted sharply at her two children running noisily ahead to stand still. "Amelia, Rubin, stop NOW!"

Frightened by the anxious tone of their mother's voice, they froze immediately, arms at their sides, shoulders down. "Momma what's wrong?" Amelia whispered in a worried voice while standing like a statue.

"Shhh!" Ina scowled at them sternly as she held her fingers to her lips. The forest was dead quiet for a few moments as if it too answered her command to be quiet. They all listened intently. Ina's heart was beating fast and she turned her head, scanning the woods that surrounded them. Then a rustle of leaves caught her attention. She focused on the direction of the noise and saw a fat gray squirrel with a big fluffy tail digging into the forest floor to bury a hickory nut in his cache.

"Oh, it's just a squirrel Momma," Rubin said, pointing toward the now chattering noisemaker. The grey squirrel had caught sight of them at the same time and was now crouched down, flattening himself low on the ground. His tail was arched over his back and he was twitching it nervously, all the while making a loud clicking noise at them.

"Did you think he was going to toss that hickory nut at us Momma?" Amelia teased and grinned. Ina's shoulders relaxed, and she exhaled a long sigh of relief as the tension of the moment changed to humor.

"Well, ya never know," she said to Amelia and Rubin, her eyes twinkling now. "He just might clim' up a tree and start hurlin' them at us. Thet could hurt you know!" She said, teasing Amelia back.

"Might even give you two a lump on your heads," and Ina shook her finger at both Amelia and Rubin. Then all three of them started laughing at the thought of a little squirrel warrior fighting them off with hickory nuts.

"You rascal, stop stealin' them nuts and git outa here!" Amelia chastised the rodent who was still making noises at them. It turned, ran off into the laurel bushes, and disappeared. The strange sense of anxiety Ina had been feeling vanished with their laughter, and she hugged them both. "We'll have to tell Papa to come over here with the gun and git us some squirrel. These rascals are fat and sassy from all these nuts. They'll make good eatin'."

Ina hadn't had much schooling. She'd met Cornelius when she was fifteen and they were married after a short courtship. She had given birth to Amelia before the first year was over. Then Rubin came three years later and now they had another baby boy, little Christopher, a one-year-old, back at the cabin with Cornelius. It was a nice sized family, small by most standards, but they were still young and she could bear him more babies. Big families were needed to work a homestead. They felt so lucky that none of their children had died from any sickness or accidents. Lots of folks lost their young to one disease or another.

Ina and the children continued through the woods to the big hickory tree she had seen, stopping at several others before going back to the cabin with their flour sacks heavy and bulging with nuts. Some of the nuts would be stored away for winter, safe from the mice, and be brought out a few at a time as a treat by the fire on a cold night. Others would be used up in cakes and cookies. They might even be able to trade some for other goods. The puffball Amelia had found was put in a safe place on the fireplace mantle for emergency use when needed. It worked great to stop nosebleeds or any bleeding cut. All you had to do was squeeze it so the brownish powder would stick to the wound and stop the flow of blood. They knew lots of ways to use the wild plants and herbs as remedies for all sorts of illnesses and emergencies.

It was late afternoon by the time they had returned. Cornelius had gotten most of the chinking patched up between the logs. He was using a combination of sticky mud and dried grasses to pack it tightly into the cracks. Soon the weather would get much worse and bitter cold winds would howl and push to get inside the cabin like an unwelcome intruder by any crack or crevice they could find. They also needed to make the cabin as air tight as possible to stay warm in the brutal winter months by sealing any openings. There was still so much to do. Ina had seen a flock of Canada geese fly over while they were crossing the field on the trip to the woods. Their long "V" shape was moving southward in the sky. Each side of the "V" was wandering and breaking up, and then coming together again. The geese were just forming a flying formation and were probably a local gaggle of many born that year and not used to flying together, so they moved up and down the ranks to find their positions in the lines. Geese that had made the trip south before usually led the way; they just had to decide on a leader and follow him.

Earlier, in the field, Ina and the children had stood still watching them, their heads turned upward toward the flock with their hands sheltering their eyes. They looked and listened to the honking of the long-necked, gray geese until they were far out of sight. Rubin even ran a ways, flapping his arms and honking, pretending he was flying with them. Ina knew that the sighting of the Canada geese heading south, the leaves turning colors, and the increasingly cooler mornings were all signs that the season was changing and warned them to pay attention. They had a good start on being ready for winter, but Ina never felt fully prepared and wanted to do more before it was too late. She would keep working until the heavy snow fell and forced her to stop. It was better to have too much than run out.

Some Pennsylvania winters were much worse than others. The snow would pile up against their door so much it was hard to push it open to go outside. Snow drifted up high against the outside of the cabin walls and blocked the daylight on the small windows last winter making them want to light a candle during the day because the cabin was so dark. Something about the cold made them want to eat more than normal too. Plus, there was always the fear of being snowed in for a long, long time and not having enough wood to keep warm or food to survive until spring.

They had planted some apple trees, but they were too small yet to bear much fruit, so they picked apples from the wild trees where they found them large enough to use. Ina had cored the apples, left the skins on, and sliced them into thin rings. Now they had strings of round apple slices suspended from the rafters of the cabin. The apples hung among bunches of herbs, mints, and other plants she'd also saved. She dried blueberries by spreading them out in the sun on a large, flat rock, and they'd also stored away red potatoes, fat orange carrots, and big, round cabbages they'd grown in the root cellar. She dried ears of corn and beans still in their shells too. Some would be rehydrated for food and others were for crop seeds next year. It had been a constant struggle to get any vegetables to harvest because of all the wild animals and birds that kept raiding their garden. Many rabbits had ended up as supper when they attempted to steal food for themselves and Cornelius caught them in the act.

Cornelius had been so busy on cabin repairs he hadn't hunted much lately, but he was going out before dawn tomorrow to see if he could get an elk or a deer for more meat to put up. Ina couldn't can much food because she didn't have the containers, and the ceramic storage crocks she needed were very hard to come by. When they had moved into this area of Pennsylvania, there was only so much they could carry with them. She'd managed a couple of large crocks and most of the basic cooking necessities, but she didn't have enough storage crocks to brine and pickle food for her growing family's needs. Most things had to be dried, salted down, or put into the root cellar to keep through the long winter months. They had dug out an area beneath the cabin floor where the root vegetables were secreted away and packed in dry grasses and moss to keep them from freezing.

There was no town store or trading post anywhere near them, or even close neighbors they could borrow from. Most people had barely enough for their own family needs anyway and not a lot to share. Occasionally a trader with packhorses would come through on his way to barter for furs with the Indians who lived way beyond them on the frontier, but that was only in good weather. During the winter months they would see no one except each other and a few hardy birds and animals venturing out into the snow looking for food. Sometimes she wondered if they had made a terrible mistake coming to this part of Pennsylvania. It was so wild and desolate, and they were so very isolated and alone.

William Penn was famous back in Harris Landing where they had come from and Ina and Cornelius knew he had negotiated a treaty with the Indians many, many years ago to get land for the settlers. He had envisioned starting a colony of settlers there he called the "Peaceful Kingdom." The Lenape* Indians had been paid for this land and had signed a treaty. The Indians weren't skilled in negotiating with the white people though and did not believe land could be owned any more than that the air could be owned. What Ina and Cornelius didn't know was that the Indians had been tricked many times by others, had already been forced to move several times, and were especially bitter about it. When the Lenape had been forced to move to lower Pennsylvania from New Jersey, they settled in the Wyoming Valley area. Then they were pushed out again because of the infamous Walking Treaty, an especially deceitful trick on the Indians.

The Indian Chiefs had agreed to sign over an amount of land one man could walk in a day and a half. It was to fulfill an old treaty that had been made with William Penn years before. They had no idea it meant ownership of the land. They thought they were just giving the whites permission to use the land for a while to share it. After William Penn returned to England, his sons and agents sold land that didn't belong to them. To force the Lenape to move off that land, they told them their ancestors had signed over as much land as could be walked in a day and a half. The Lenape thought that meant the white man would walk along the river for a few miles, sit down, smoke a pipe, and maybe now and then shoot a squirrel, but not to have kept running all day.

The sly land agents took advantage of the vagueness of the terms, hiring three fast runners and clearing paths ahead of them so they could cover a tremendous amount of land in the allotted time the Indians had agreed to. That area was further multiplied when the new boundary lines were drawn from the point where the last man stopped in a northeast direction on over to join the boundary on the Delaware River. Then another boundary line was drawn back down to the beginning point, making a huge triangle to

---

* Per the Nanticoke and Lenape Confederation, the preferred pronunciation for the name of this tribe is Le-NAH-pay.

include thousands of acres of fertile land. It was approximately the size of Rhode Island. The land that was lost in the Walking Treaty had been prime, ancestral Indian territory full of game and had pure mountain streams abounding with fish and beaver.

It was much more land than the Indians ever intended to sign away, but the treaty stood according to the Pennsylvania Authorities despite the anger and protests of the many Indians who were affected and displaced. The Lenape too felt they had to honor the treaty their forefathers had signed and did what they were told. Of course, the land agents failed to disclose the fact that the Indians had been tricked out of the land to people like Ina and Cornelius. They, like the other new settlers, thought the Lenape were all in agreement with the treaty, had been compensated well, and had willingly and peacefully moved away.

CHAPTER 2

I T HAD BEEN A SCARY AND courageous decision for Ina and Cornelius to leave the comforts of living close to town and head out to start a new life on the frontier. At first, the road north was well worn and not that difficult to travel. Horses' hooves and wagon wheels from others before them had pounded down the earth into solid footing. They had waited until after the early rainy season so they would have fewer problems with the wheels getting bogged down in mud. Eventually though, the wide track became very narrow and tall grass and brush became denser between the rutted tracks. Boulders jutted up here and there and tree roots and dangerous narrow passageways became more common on the rocky terrain. In some places along the streams, the earth was slippery and swampy for their wagon, and they could see where others before them had put down logs to help the wagons cross those wet areas. But further along, there was nothing to help and they just had to do the best they could to navigate through. Sometimes the route disappeared into tall clumps of ferns and brush higher than the wheel hubs and it was hard to find the trail at all.

After traveling for several days over all types of terrain, they reached a blockhouse. The building was just a crude square log cabin solidly built of unhewn pine logs. A burly man named Tag stepped out of the rough frame doorway and called out to them.

"I run this here stop. Cim on in, sit and talk a spell," he said. His livelihood, as it became known to Ina and Cornelius, was "helpin' ta outfit travlers," he told them.

The interior of the room was dark and smelled like a combination of smoke and an animal stable. All sorts of tools, pots and pans, lanterns, woodsman's clothes, and miscellaneous food stuffs hung down from rafters and were on spikes on the interior walls of the room. Wooden wagon wheels were propped up in one corner along with shovels and axes and toothy saws. Dried corn and other seeds were heaped in containers here and there. There wasn't any organization as to where items were placed. It was clear that he lived there alone.

Tag asked Ina and Cornelius, "What's ya doin' here, and where abouts your'n headin?"

They filled him in on their background and that they were headed up north to start a homestead.

"Yep, I knowed that," he said as if he'd heard the same story several times already.

He motioned for them to sit on some of the wooden barrels that held provisions. He went and got two banged up tin cups and poured them some kind of strong tea from a blackened metal pot. It tasted kind of minty and also like the pot had never been cleaned. He told them it was made from roasted dandelion roots and mint leaves. Ina noticed his hands were blackened like the pot and wondered if he ever washed them even though there was soap for sale there. They sipped their drinks slowly, enjoying the break from the rough wagon ride, and talked with him, hoping to get more solid information on what was ahead of them yet. They wanted him to verify their dreams of what could be waiting for them. Tag took a big knife out of a leather sheaf he wore and started digging dirt from under his fingernails. "Yep," he nodded his head. "There's lots of land up there fer anyone who kin do the back breakin' work ta clearing. Lots of folks are settlin" up in there. All kinds of folks, old 'uns and young 'uns even some furiners. Theys all headin' up thet a way," he said.

"Not me, I got it good herin. When they git thet plank road out here built I'm gonna be in all kinds of money." he said gesturing toward the rude dirt wagon tracks that ran in front of the blockhouse door. "Theys gonna put planks down right up thru them hills. It'll be like takin' a fancy carriage ride. Then folks 'ill be a comin' thru here all the time. I'll be rich. Mite even git me a woman to cook and clean fer me and keep me warm at night." He laughed and winked at them. Ina winced at the thought of living with Tag. He smelled like the stacks of animal furs piled up around the edges of the room. His dull, greasy hair and tangled beard were clumped together and scraggly looking. His clothing was stiff with worn-in old dirt. A wad of tobacco was bulging in his cheek and she watched as he spit juice onto the floor. He'd done that so much a shiny brown patina was built up on the floor's boards. The small stream of brown liquid slithered down between the cracks in the floorboards like an escaping snake. His teeth also showed the stains and glinted tan with brown crevices when he smiled. He had the annoying habit of leaning close to talk and jabbing his stiff finger into your shoulder to punctuate his words.

Their two children had been poking through some of the miscellaneous junk around them and feeling the soft furs from strange animals they didn't know. They admired a wolf's skin now complete with its head and fangs showing. They were touching and petting the pelts of fur piled up on a table when suddenly one fur moved. It raised its head, showed its teeth, and made a noise at them. Startled, they screamed and ran back to Ina and Cornelius. Tag started laughing hard and pounding his hand on his knee.

"Gotch ya didn't he!" Tag could hardly talk he was laughing so hard. "Oh, thets jest my 'coon, he won't hurt ya. Durn thing lays about all day and gits up at night. I caught him when he was a young'n. See he's got some toes gone. Was gunna bash him in the head but thought no I'll let him grow some. More fur then. Now, I keep 'em round for compny. Durn thing!" Amelia and Rubin leaned in closer to their parents.

Tag invited Ina and Cornelius to camp by the blockhouse that night. They were tired and seriously considering it, but two seedy looking trappers came into the blockhouse that made them reconsider that idea. Tag was also getting to be even more repulsive and overly friendly. Ina was uncomfortable with the way he kept talking in her face with his rank, steamy breath, and Cornelius didn't like the way he was paying so much attention to Ina either. Now these two other rough looking men were in the room too. She pressed Cornelius's arm in a signal urging him to leave. He understood her message; he'd had enough of Tag also. Amelia and Rubin had wandered off to explore some more and Cornelius called to them as he stood up and thanked Tag for the tea and hospitality.

"Yer stayin' the night, ain't ya?" he asked. "Don't you need some vittles or tools? Yer jest got here!" Tag said. "Cim, look at this rifle I got over herin," and he pulled at Cornelius' sleeve.

"No, not this time. We best be gitten on our way, got a lot of ground to cover yet," Cornelius answered back. If he needed something he could always travel back to the blockhouse another time, he thought. He didn't know at that time how far he would go from that place before he found his land.

Ina thanked Tag also and gratefully headed outside for a breath of fresh air. Tag was still trying to sell Cornelius a fancy rifle, but he reassured him that his was perfectly fine and quickly escaped out the door when the trappers asked Tag for something. The family climbed back into the wagon and before long they were on their way again. Both were silently hoping all the people they met from now on were not going to be like Tag and the other trappers.

When they headed out from Harris Landing, they passed by other homesteads where families had already gotten a good start on their building. They even had crops planted between the cut off stumps of fallen trees and livestock grazing in rude fence enclosures made of saplings and brush. Ina and Cornelius wondered if any good land would be left for them to claim. It seemed as if all the unclaimed free land they saw now consisted of rocky ravines and craggy soilless hilltops. In other places, the dark woods and laurel were so thick it would take forever just to hack out a clearing for the cabin, let alone for letting sun in to start crops. So, they kept pushing northward in the small wagon stuffed with all their personal belongings.

They were impressed by all the game they saw while they were travelling. Huge flocks of wild turkeys were feeding on grass and bugs. Quail and pheasants rose and took flight as the wagon passed. Startled groups of deer and elk bounded away from them and whenever they came close to a stream or pond, it was populated with mallards and Canada geese, ducks they didn't know the names for, muskrat, and beaver. Cornelius soon felt even more confident he could hunt and provide for his family. There was food here for the taking and fur he could trap and trade for goods they would need in the future.

Cornelius kept his eyes open for any game that would also make a meal as they travelled north. Rabbits darted ahead of them and he was quick to shoot one for supper. He cleaned and skinned it, and Ina roasted it on a stick over the open fire. She also boiled up some potatoes to go with it. They camped each night at dusk, ate, and then stared into their campfire, hoping that tomorrow they'd find their land, their dream place. They talked of what they would do first and how long it would take them to get settled in.

Cornelius told them all, "Look up at them stars . . . they're shinin' down on our new home somewhere. Maybe we'll find it tomorrow."

While traveling, they'd eat a simple breakfast, often just boiled oatmeal and a drink, and head north again, bumping along all day, taking turns riding and walking. In the evening they'd sit around and look at the stars and dream some more, talking about what they were going to do when they got to their homestead. They planned how the rooms would be set up and what size the cabin had to be and what they had to accomplish the first year. They talked of crops to plant and animals they would need for food and working the land, and how nice it would be to have a home to call their own. Then they would fall asleep and rise the next day to travel on. Finally, after they travelled a very long distance and crossed through that last narrow river valley and went up a rise leaving the last new homestead they saw far, far behind them, they found the place they wanted to make their home. It had woods full of straight trees for building and they saw a fresh water spring and some open areas where deer were grazing oblivious of their presence. Their long, tiring journey north had ended. Now their new life and the real work would begin.

It took a while and some discussions for Cornelius and Ina to decide exactly where to put the cabin they would build. This new land already had an open field the forest hadn't claimed yet, or perhaps it was an area that had been cleared by a lightning sparked fire many years before. Cornelius had wanted the cabin set back in the woods to save the open field for crops. It was an awful, backbreaking job to cut trees and pull out stumps with a horse and chain and clear a field for planting. Usually the first-year trees got cut off for logs to build with and you had to plant crops between the cutoff stumps, so they felt fortunate they had found an area with an open place for planting. Ina wanted the cabin in the open field so the sun would be on it and it wouldn't be so dark inside, but they both agreed they should leave the open land for crops and grazing for their animals.

They set up a rough camp and slept in the wagon for many weeks before a small cabin was raised. Ina used an axe to limb the trees that Cornelius fell and pulled her end of the crosscut saw with all the strength she could muster. Sometimes Cornelius pulled the saw back so hard it came right out of her hands. Every night they lay down with sore muscles, blistered hands, and bone-tired bodies. With the help of the horse, levers and ropes, and the push of the dream in their hearts, they raised their cabin walls. It was small, very rough, but functional. They also added a lean-to on the side for the horse and wood storage. They would build a proper barn for their livestock and wagon next year, Cornelius promised. Their new homestead wasn't fancy looking; it was really kind of homely in its crudeness, but it was theirs and it could grow into the dream they shared in their hearts.

In the end, Ina and Cornelius had compromised and built their cabin at the edge of the clearing facing south, so the morning sun shone on the front walls each day and sunlight came in the two small square windows. That way when they were stuck inside the cabin due to bad weather or the bitter cold of winter, Ina would still see sunshine coming in her windows and they would have light to read or work by.

They had been so busy getting the homestead going and excited about the promise of it that they had little time to think of family and friends left behind. Winter was the time for that, when you were shut in for many days away from everything that normally occupied you from sunup to sundown. Winter was the time to think about how far they had come and what they could hope for at the end of their first crop season and every season after that.

That first winter was a brutal learning experience. Snow came early and lasted way into spring. The frigid winds pried their way through gaps in the chinking they didn't know they had. They were constantly plugging the spaces between the logs to try and keep the snow out and the warmth inside. The wood fire had to be kept piled high with burning logs to battle the plunging temperatures outdoors.

Time passed, Ina and Cornelius were proud of what they had built with their own hands in just a couple years. They had staked out a large area of land around them for future use and gotten it registered with an agent. They also built that barn they talked about for the livestock and more out-buildings as well. Another lean-to was added onto the cabin for storing more wood under cover from winter and have a sheltered place for Cornelius and Ina to split the blocks down into burnable chunks with an axe. And they had put a lot of work into making their cabin more livable. It was such a pleasant woodsy cabin. The large, open main room had a big stone fireplace on its back wall for cooking and heating. Cornelius had hauled the flat, gray stones all the way from a creek using the horse and a stone bolt to drag them across the field, making several trips. He laid them up in a stone fireplace wall that went clear to the ceiling and through the roof. He had squared off a hand-hewn maple beam with a drawknife and used it for the mantel piece over the cooking area of the hearth. He used his pocket knife to carve a cross in the center of the mantle and carved the initials I.B. on one side and C.B. on the other side to bring blessings to their little home.

The area beside and behind the fireplace was divided into two more small rooms. One was a tiny kitchen storage area for supplies, cooking pots and pans, and food put up for the winter months. The other was a small bedroom where Cornelius and Ina could have some privacy. One corner of it doubled as an indoor privy to be used during bad weather. A bar of homemade lye soap rested on a slab wood shelf along with a metal pan of water and a flour sack hand towel. They had a bucket to use when needed for a privy and a cloth curtain strung on a rope. The rest of the time, in good weather, they all had to go outdoors to use the outhouse in the back. That was a miserable trip if they had to go in the night, rain or snow; plus, there was the added danger of snakes or wild animals prowling around at night, so the makeshift indoor privy was a necessity.

The children all slept in the "big room" where all the cooking and daily activities happened when they weren't outdoors. Their rustic cots, made of tree saplings, were along the walls and served as sitting furniture for reading and playing games. The floors in the house were all rough-hewn, plank boards, a luxury a lot of homesteaders didn't have, but Cornelius took the time to see that their cabin did. Earth floors were common in most cabins, but that made them damp, cold, and dirty, so they wanted plank for their cabin. The children had made drawings with charcoal on some papery bark from white birch and pinned them up on the rounded log walls. Cornelius was good at making the family rustic furniture and Rubin and Amelia both had low stools they could sit on by the fire. He had even crafted a little bed for their youngest child Christopher, who was too small to take along hickory nut gathering that day and had stayed behind with his Papa instead. Ina had brought her rocking chair north and Cornelius had made himself a sturdy man's chair.

All the beds in the house had quilts that were pieced from fabric scraps and old clothes. They weren't fancy quilt designs, just different colored squares sewn together. But Ina had a way of combining the colors and patterns that made them attractive. They looked like checkerboards with each square a different color or pattern and were a pleasure to see as well as being cozy to sleep under. They brightened the otherwise drab looking interior of brown logs and wood boards. The window curtains were made of coarse muslin flour sacks. It was hard to keep them looking nice because the smoke of the cooking fire and candles burning darkened everything. In the evening they lit the beeswax candles, which gave off a circle of light. That light, along with the fire that flickered and sparked, gave the big room a magical warm and close feeling. When they added pine cones or pine logs onto the fire, the whole room smelled of the sweet forest.

On the mantle was a collection of various kinds of pinecones the children had collected. The long, narrow ones with the sticky white sap were from the large, stately Eastern White pines so abundant in the forest where they lived. They had used mostly white pine logs and boards for their cabin. They were plentiful and a long-lasting wood that gave off their piney scent when cut. The smallest pinecones, about the size of a grape, were from the hemlock trees that were also plentiful. The native wild turkeys loved those pinecones and became easy targets for Cornelius when the cones covered the ground under the trees. The big birds busied themselves scratching among them and eating the small seeds so they didn't pay attention to man or beast stalking them. Quite often they could hear the turkeys calling from the woods and see flocks of them come into the field hunting insects and seeds in the grass. Their brown feathers flashed with metallic blue, green, and bronze colors in the sun. The tom turkey was almost comical when he puffed himself up big, spread his tail, and strutted around showing off for the hens.

Rubin had found half of a discarded deer antler that a mouse had chewed on when they were in the woods and brought that home. The mouse had made tiny toothy gouges all along as it chewed it like an ear of corn, and that was laying on the mantle now too. Amelia had found a rock with the fossil of a seashell in it, which made her wonder how it had gotten there so far from the ocean that she had heard about. Ina had placed some stems of late blooming Witch Hazel in a small vase. She'd picked them off the scraggly tree by a wet area. Though their blooms weren't much, just a few spidery petals of yellow, they were about the only thing left blooming this late in the year.

Along the side of the fireplace hanging on pegs made from cut off tree branches were some husked ears of corn that had a few colored kernels in them. The dark kernels stood out in the perfect rows of golden yellow corn like toothy gaps. Also in the room was a small table that Cornelius had made from a thick slab of pine. A hand painted, wooden checkerboard sat on top of it now, with checkers made of corncob slices. Half of the checkers were colored black with soot, the others left plain. Amelia and her father had quite a match going, and it still hadn't been decided who was the better checker player.

Ina gave Amelia a lot of credit. She was a bright girl with a mind of her own and was so curious about the woods and wild things. If Ina or Cornelius couldn't answer her questions about the workings of nature, Amelia would go out and study it until she figured it out for herself. One time she wanted to know about polliwogs. She kept asking Ina and Cornelius the same questions: what happened first, did they get their legs then their tail fell off? Or did their tail fall off and then they grew their legs? Neither Ina nor Cornelius knew, so Amelia went out and got some frog eggs from a boggy area nearby, brought them home quickly in her apron pocket, and put them in an enameled pan with some water. Then she watched the clear gelatinous mass with its little black specks for weeks. Finally, they turned from black dots in the eggs to baby frogs with kicking green legs. After they grew their legs, their tail disappeared. Her curiosity satisfied, she took them back to the bog where they belonged and let them loose. She had found her answer; she never kept wild things as pets for long. They only visited for a short time. She treasured the wildness of the animals and birds and wouldn't think of depriving them of their freedom.

Ina put the full sacks of hickory nuts back into the small storage room behind the stone fireplace. It made her feel better to know they had more food for winter. Then she went back outside to talk to Cornelius and check on Christopher. They had named their youngest son Christopher because they had traveled to a strange land where he was born in the early autumn. It was a remote part of the new world Columbus had traveled to, so they thought the name was appropriate. Every pioneer knew the story of Christopher Columbus and passed it on to their children. Cornelius was packing the last bit of mud and dried grasses between the rows of pine logs up under the eaves and looked a mess where he had wiped his sweaty brow with his mud splattered arms. Ina could see he'd also used his trousers for a towel and they were streaked with mud all down the front of the pant legs. She'd have to do some heavy scrubbing on the washboard with lye soap to get them clean. He was doing necessary dirty work so she expected and tolerated the very dirty clothes.

Christopher had gotten muddy too and was busy patting together a mud and grass cookie out of what fell to the ground where he was sitting. Mud was squishing out between his small fingers and it was smeared on his chubby cheeks. He had pieces of muddy grass stuck in his hair and Ina couldn't help but laugh at the sight of both of them. She glanced up at the chinking.

"Lookin' good Cornelius," she said, smiling up at him on the ladder. He nodded his head at her and asked how the hickory nut crop was this year. "Well it'd be better if those darn squirrels didn't beat me to so many. It took a while, but we got some sacks full," she replied. She bent over to pick Christopher up and groaned at how heavy he was getting for a one-year-old. He must weigh about eighteen to twenty pounds now, she thought. Ina had been concerned when she hadn't gotten pregnant after they started homesteading, but then after some time she discovered she was expecting and they all happily anticipated the birth of their first child to be born in the wilderness. She hadn't had any complications giving birth to Amelia or Rubin. Fortunately, the new baby's birth went well. Christopher arrived with the help of Cornelius, healthy and squalling loudly to the delight of his sister and brother. Ina was so glad he was strong and healthy now, and not frail and slight like Rubin.

She worried about that boy; a man had to be physically strong to survive in these wilds and make a homestead for his family. It wasn't something you could hire someone to do for you out here; you had to do your own hard work. She wished Rubin would start growing faster, put some weight on, and be sturdy like Amelia. Then, turning her thoughts back to her day in the woods she said to Cornelius, "There's lots of fat squirrels over that way if you're fixin' to get some meat."

"Well I'll shoot some, but later on, they're close by and I kin shake them out of the nest and shoot 'em even when the snow starts," he answered. "I think I should go out and git us a deer though like we talked, maybe even an elk, so we kin put up more meat afore the snow starts driftin' and I can't git far away to hunt. I was thinkin' I'd go out afore you get up in the mornin'." He finished up what he was doing and backed on down the ladder. "Probably over to thet bog area where their eatin' on thet green grass," he added. "I've seen 'em over thet way lately."

Ina agreed they did need more meat, and although she'd miss his company, it was a common understanding on the frontier that the men had to go off hunting, sometimes for days. The women were expected to stay home and take care of the children, feed the livestock, and keep the fire going. Game moved around and weren't always that close to the cabin, especially now in the rutting season when they travelled more. Ina took Christopher inside to clean up before supper and Cornelius quit chinking and joined them.

Ina was tired, but her work for the day wasn't done yet. There was still supper to make, dishes to do, and children to get cleaned up and off to bed before she could rest. Amelia was a big help to her and knew how to make biscuits by herself now, so she got busy making them. Cornelius had killed an old hen earlier and cleaned it for Ina, so she put some cut up chicken in a cast iron pot with some water, potatoes, and salt and set it in the fire close to the embers. Then she piled some coals on the lid and left it. She washed some greens she had picked and set them to boil too. It was a good meal and they enjoyed some of the hickory nuts for dessert while joking about that "dangerous" squirrel. Then Cornelius and Amelia spent time together playing checkers. Ina sewed for a while with the sewing kit she had inherited when her mother passed away. It was just a little, round, dark wicker basket with a hinged lid decorated with some small colorful beads. Inside it held a pincushion, thread and needles, and a beautiful embossed silver thimble her mother had used. It had delicate little raised flowers decorating it along with her mother's initials. It had been a gift from her father to her mother one Christmas and she still remembered their faces when they exchanged gifts that morning so long ago. When she put the treasured thimble on her finger she felt like she was touching her mother's hand again. Ina wanted to get started on making some presents for Christmas before it was too late into autumn and worked on her sewing whenever she had a chance. The checker game ended with Amelia winning this time and then the children were sent to bed.

Ina had taken the children to church meetings back in Harris Landing and was missing them being taught by a real preacher. However, she had brought her family bible to read and teach the stories to them. This night she read to Amelia and Rubin about Moses's escape from Egypt into the desert. Amelia, always curious, asked, "What's a desert Momma?" It was hard for Ina to explain something she had never seen herself. She told them it was fields and mountains of just sand and no water or forest or game anywhere. "I don't want to live there!" Amelia said, and Rubin shook his little head no also.

"You never have to Amelia, you can live here as long as you want to and maybe someday you kin have your own cabin near us when you marry," Ina told her.

"No momma, I don't want to ever leave. I want to stay here with you and Papa!" Amelia was almost sobbing.

"Shush now," Ina said hugging her. "It's alright sweetie, you can live with us as long as you want. Now go to sleep and dream of that white pony you've always wanted." Ina tucked them all in; Amelia and Rubin slept in the same bed. Christopher, who slept in his own little bed, had fallen fast asleep earlier.

Cornelius poked here and there around the cabin, gathered his hunting things together and checked out his gun and the powder supply in his powder horns. He liked to keep two full horns in readiness for shooting his flintlock rifle. He set out everything he needed to hunt with in the morning. Ina decided to quit for the night and set her sewing aside. Cornelius banked up the fire by raking the coals together and laying some large logs on it to last the night. They both blew out the beeswax candles, said goodnight to the sleepy children already tucked in bed, and went into their small bedroom. The embers in the fireplace let off a warm, rosy glow and sparked like tiny shooting stars once and awhile, and that kept the cabin dimly lit and cozy at night. The tired children soon fell fast asleep. They were worn out from their hiking and working that day too. All was peaceful, cozy, and warm at their homestead in the woods.

Ina awoke briefly very late in the night to the sound of coyotes singing somewhere off in the moonlight. She noticed Cornelius was gone from bed already. She had been sleeping so soundly she hadn't felt him get up. She quietly got up to peek at the children in the big room to see if they were all still covered up. Rubin had kicked the quilt off and when she pulled it back over him he woke, drowsy eyed, and asked to come sleep in her bed. She lifted his small body into her arms and carried him into her room. Looking back into the big room, she noticed Cornelius's gun and powder horn were gone off the rack by the front door. Now she knew for sure he'd gone out early to hunt as he planned. She tucked Rubin under the covers, kissed his forehead, and stroked his hair. He instantly closed his eyes and drifted off. Soon Ina fell back to sleep too with Rubin's small body snuggling against her.

CHAPTER 3

INA HAD JUST STARTED HAVING A pleasant dream about their homestead when suddenly, violently, she was being pulled out of bed. Someone had grabbed both her feet and dragged her with a painful thud onto the rough plank floor. Rubin had also been jerked out of bed that way and now cried loudly, terribly frightened and clinging to her. Standing above them was an Indian with a menacing war club in his hand. Part of his face was painted red and black, and he was dressed in clothing made from deer skins. His hair was straight and jet black like the color of a raven. His feet, which were in front of Ina and Rubin's faces, had moccasins on them with high tops that were fringed just below his knees. Ina looked up at the angry face hovering over her and was horrified to see both his earlobes had been slit open. It was an old wound, but the flesh hung down like a cruel gaping smile on each side of his face. Loops of beads on strings were threaded through the slits and hung as earrings from them. He reached down and lifted Ina and Rubin roughly by one arm and jerked them to their feet. Ina quickly silenced Rubin by pulling him close to her where he hid his face. Then the Indian shoved them both into the big room.

Amelia was standing by her cot and quietly crying. Ina saw terror in her eyes when they looked at each other. Amelia held onto Christopher and rocked him back and forth to calm him. Christopher reached out to Ina as soon as he saw his mother and she instinctively took him in her arms and drew all the children close to her body to protect them. Rubin turned his face away from the Indian and wrapped his arms tightly around his mother's knees. There was another Indian in the room, a taller, bigger man. He was dressed much the same as the other and had the same long black hair, only with a topknot and a couple eagle feathers sticking out of it. He also had earlobes with the same big gaping slits in them. She recognized their style of dress from a description she had heard of the Lenape Indians. Unknown to her, they were part of the group that had been pushed from New Jersey, and then again by the Walking Purchase so settlers could move in. The bigger Indian was ransacking the cabin now, collecting things into a pillowcase he had taken off the children's bed.

Ina was terror stricken but appeared outwardly calm for her children. Fear for them quickened her breath and all her senses were magnified as she tried to understand what was happening and anticipate what might happen next. The door to the cabin was swung wide open and cold air was blowing in on them. When Cornelius had gone out, no one had been up to bolt the door shut. Ina and Cornelius had never really felt the need to be that vigilant about locking things up tight. They thought the Indian problem had been resolved long ago because the land agents had sworn to them it was safe to homestead where they were. They hadn't had any trouble since they started their homestead years earlier and had felt safe. *Why have they broken into our cabin now and are so angry?* she wondered.

Ina tried speaking English to them. In a firm, authoritative voice she said, "My husband will be right back with some other men who went huntin' with him. They have a lot of guns." The smaller Indian leaned close toward her and raised his club, threatening to strike her. Ina understood it meant not to speak. Both Indians were pointing at items in the cabin now, talking quickly to each other and picking up things to stuff into the ticking pillowcases.

She couldn't understand their words, but their gesturing motions were clear. She watched them warily and hugged her children even closer. Her few treasures, some colorful ribbons, loose buttons, and some wooden matches were shoved into the pillow cases along with the sewing kit she had been using the night before. She thought briefly of her mother's silver thimble tucked away inside the darkness of the little wicker basket. The smaller Indian took what few kitchen knives they had and some small cooking pots. They also grabbed the leftover biscuits and dried apple slices that hung from the rafters. When they got all they could stuff into the cases they looked around wistfully as if wishing they could find more. The big Indian grabbed the frightened family's cloaks off the pegs on the wall and held them out toward Ina. She stood there not quite understanding what he wanted.

Her mind had been spinning full of questions as they robbed and ransacked the cabin around her. Where was Cornelius now? Did he get away? Did they wait to come in until they saw him leave in the dark to go hunting, or did they kill him after he left the cabin? She couldn't dwell on that now. She had to focus on what the Indian was trying to tell her to do. He was poking hard at her shoulder with his finger, acting as if she were stupid as he shook the cloaks in her face. He gestured for them to put them on. She wanted to get dressed, not just put her cloak on, as she was only in her night clothes. *What were they going to do with us? Why did he want our cloaks on?* Questions were racing through her head.

She didn't want to leave her cabin. She shook her head "no" at the Indian, all the time keeping her eyes on his face and stroking the children's heads. The big one, with his face painted half black, grabbed Amelia's arm forcefully and started shoving her into her cloak to show what he wanted saying, "Ilka tòtun!"

Amelia pulled away and cried, "Don't touch me!" But he was being so rough and forceful that Ina quickly pushed his hand away and said sharply, "All right, all right. We'll put them on." *If I don't do what they want*, she thought, *they might kill us all right here.*

It was actually a good omen that they wanted them to put on cloaks, she thought. *Maybe they don't intend to hurt us.* So she quickly bundled up the children as best she could while being pushed, shoved, and hurried by the two Indian men. She barely had time to help Amelia and Rubin get their shoes on and put on her own cloak. She was still trying to get Christopher wrapped in a blanket when they were all forced out the door and down the narrow, worn path that went out into the woods. She looked back and realized they were all traveling away from the direction Cornelius would have gone to hunt that morning. *How would Cornelius know which way we've headed*, she asked herself, so she started scuffing her feet as she walked when the Indians weren't looking.

The children soon sensed that they should be quiet and only spoke briefly in whispers to her. She quickly shushed them and told them calmly, "Everything will be all right, Momma's here." They all walked single file; the big Indian was leading, then Amelia behind him, followed by Ina carrying Christopher, then Rubin, and the smaller Indian was last. He was the more frightening one to look at, with those big dangling slits in his earlobes and black tattooed patterns on his body where it wasn't covered by animal skins. As they walked briskly, she listened to the few words they spoke, trying to figure out by their tone what was going on. She didn't sense anger in their words now, just a sound of urgency. Mostly they were silent though or gestured to each other with hand signals. They were moving at a brisk pace, trying to get some distance away from the cabin as soon as possible. Once, they halted suddenly and the Indian with the red and black painted face had the family crouch down low. He forced them to be silent by intimidating them with his war club again. Ina never saw what had startled the Indians, but after a while the lead one motioned for Ina and the children to get back up and head off again.

They walked in that fashion, single file, for a long time at a fast, steady pace. Once Rubin said loudly, "Momma I'm hungry," and she had to quiet him again. Christopher was heavy and restless in her arms. She had to keep shifting his weight from side to side and balancing him on her hip. She had figured out that the large Indian with the black face paint was called Constayunka. The smaller one was named something that sounded like Shomachsom, she thought. It was hard to carry Christopher as it was, but Shomachsom had also tied two of her small metal pots together on a string and put them over her head, and that was weighing her down even more. They kept tangling up and banging against her with every step she took. They traveled on through the woods as fast as they could, all the while going on an incline, and by late that morning they stopped on the plateau of a mountain. Here, Constayunka and Shomachsom dumped out the contents of the pillowcases while keeping an eye on their captives. Then they started going through the things they'd stolen at the cabin. Ina saw they were splitting up their newly pillaged possessions and was troubled about what might happen next.

The children were very tired and hungry, not having had breakfast. Amelia and the baby seemed to be holding up well, but Ina was concerned about little Rubin. There was no way she could carry him and Christopher and hoped they wouldn't be forced to cover too much distance that day. Constayunka finished dividing up their plunder and doubled back along the way they had just come. He was checking to see if they were being followed. While he was gone Shomachsom kept a close, suspicious watch on all the captives, especially Ina. His staring gaze made her feel very uneasy, and she found herself wishing Constayunka would return soon. Shomachsom was getting restless and Ina was awfully nervous about being left alone with the smaller, more dangerous acting Indian. He kept playing with a butcher knife he had taken from her cabin. He had her favorite one in his hands now. Cornelius had made it for Ina from a broken saw blade. It had been a Christmas gift to her and still shone beautifully from the careful way he crafted, ground, and polished it. He had even inlaid a penny into the black cherry handle he'd carved. He told her, "Ya always give someone a penny with a knife so it don't cut the friendship." She watched Shomachsom pry the lucky penny out and study both sides of it.

Constayunka returned looking satisfied and motioned them all to stand up and get moving. The group set off at a swift pace again. The walking was difficult now because the terrain was uneven and the ground where they stepped was rocky and rutted from many deer tracks and tree roots. Rubin was walking slower and slower, his frail body and thin legs getting very tired, and Shomachsom started giving Rubin a shove on his small back whenever he slowed down. They were still traveling single file through the woods, as it was the only way to get through the brush and trees. Rubin started falling now, and each time Ina cringed as Shomachsom would jerk him back to his feet by his small arm and push him onward down the narrow trail yelling angry words at him. Amelia wanted to boost him up onto her back, but they wouldn't even pause to let her do that. Ina kept encouraging him on when she could, despite stern words from both the Indians in their own language to be quiet. The group was going down the side of a ravine on a steep deer path between large flat boulders the size of tables. The path was slippery with all the loose shale lying on it that had dropped down from the wet and dripping rock outcroppings. The path narrowed even more and on one side the land dropped sharply away and downward. Suddenly, Rubin lost his footing and fell sideways down over the high cliff and out of sight into the ravine below. She could hear him cry out and then his body hitting obstacles as he fell even further. Ina let out a horrible scream that echoed back from the dark, gray cliff walls and mountains of hardwoods. Shomachsom gave her such a solid hit to her head and face with his fist that she fell on the ground and lay there unconscious still holding onto Christopher.

Ina woke sometime later with her captors poking and kicking at her with their feet. She sat upright, picked up the baby who was sitting beside her, and looked blankly at them, dazed and confused, trying to remember what had happened but aware that her face was very tender and swollen. Shomachsom pulled her harshly to her feet and pushed her forward down the trail, not giving her a chance to look behind her. Constayunka was still leading the way, with Amelia behind him, then Ina, but when Ina turned to look behind her, all she saw was Shomachsom. There was no sign of her little Rubin anywhere. She tried to call his name but her mouth and jaw hurt so badly she could barely make noises. Amelia sobbed, "He's dead Momma, he's dead." Ina's head was exploding with pain and her chest ached with grief. A new awareness for how dangerous their situation was made her concentrate and focus harder on saving Amelia and Christopher. She couldn't think clearly, but instinctively she knew they were all in grave danger and she had to protect her other children from harm. With heavy grief and fear, she kept moving forward one step at a time.

The light was changing and Ina could tell it was now late afternoon. They were walking along a creek bottom among swaying limber willows and strong, towering cottonwood trees. Ina thought she knew this creek but didn't recall this spot and realized they were already a long way from home. The Indians stopped momentarily again, and everyone had a chance to get a drink of the cold creek water. Ina had to hold the water in her cupped hand so Christopher could have a drink too. He wasn't used to drinking out of a cup yet because she still nursed him, but he managed to swallow some of the water. Amelia came over and buried her face in Ina's cloak. All Ina could do was hug her, brush her hair back from her sad eyes, and bend over and kiss her forehead for comfort.

The Indians didn't allow them to speak to each other. She was proud of the strength Amelia was showing. She had always been such a tomboy, constantly running through the fields and climbing trees, stubborn and independent but willing to do hard work without complaining. Those qualities were keeping her alive now, though she didn't know it. Constayunka pointed toward the way they should go and motioned for them to stand up to get going again. Ina got the metal pots tangled around her neck and Christopher when she tried to stand. They were twisted and choking her, and she was angry at the fact that Shomachsom made her carry them. She managed to get untangled, lifted the string holding the pots over her head, and threw them off.

Shomachsom saw what she did, walked over, picked them up and roughly put them back over Ina's head. Then he put his face so close to hers they almost touched noses. He glared into her eyes with hatred and steamy words admonished her in Lenape that implied that she carries them or else! Then he walked away. Ina became angrier and more defiant at his treatment. She took the pots off again and flung them down, only further away this time. Shomachsom had been watching her and again glared menacingly at her. He went to where the pots lay on the ground, picked them up and again put them over Ina's head. Then he let go a stream of Indian obscenities while waving his fist and club in the air. After he had vented his anger, he turned his back and walked away. He expected her to comply and follow his orders, but she refused. Ina was now blindly, recklessly furious and was determined not to carry the pots for anyone, anywhere, especially this contemptible savage.

For the third time she took them off and threw them as far as she could, shouting, "No . . . I will not carry them ever!" Then she closed her eyes and expected to be struck with a painful blow to her head. Shomachsom was now totally enraged; he rushed over, retrieved the pots, and returned to Ina with cruel intentions. His eyes were narrowed as he strode back to her and flexed his muscles with each determined step. Constayunka stopped him just as he reached Ina and an argument between them ensued. She could tell Shomachsom was not happy about what Constayunka was saying. He tried to shove Constayunka out of the way to get at Ina, but the larger Indian was persistent and was able to keep Shomach-som under control. Shomachsom gave in and put the pots over his own shoulder, all the while giving Ina murderous looks. Finally, he turned and hesitantly walked away, muttering under his breath.

Constayunka stepped closer to Ina and said in English, "You are a good squaw, he is nulhàt, he can carry them." That was when she realized at least one of them spoke some English, and also that she was now probably considered property of her protector.

Ina reached out and grabbed his arm as he turned away from her. He suddenly froze in his steps. She wanted to question him about their intentions for her and her children. He looked down at her hand as if he had been touched by something unclean and shook it off. He only paused briefly, then went back to talking in Indian language and gestured to her to be quiet. Discouraged, her arm hung limp at her side. He wasn't going to allow any communi-cation between them. There was no way she could convince him to let them go.

Ina thought they had just stopped at the creek to get a drink, but Constayunka motioned them all to move on and pushed her and Amelia into the shallow water to cross the stream. It was cold and slippery going. Some of the submerged rocks were covered with fine green moss. The creek bottom was rocky, and it was hard to tell if the next step you took was going to be on the same level or down into a deeper hole. Icy springs from high in the mountains fed the creek and that kept the almost freezing water biting cold and swift. The water level got deeper out toward the middle of the stream and was quite high on Amelia. Constayunka half carried, half dragged Amelia through the deepest part to keep her from completely falling in. Ina's woolen cloak became a sodden, heavy weight dragging her down and she had to hold Christopher up high to cross the deepest part and keep him dry.

They reached the opposite shore and were now deep into the uncivilized Indian country beyond the edge of the settler's frontier. The Indians let them wring water from their clothes and dump it out of their shoes. Even so, the hems of the coarse, homespun ma-terial kept dripping and the garments hung heavy on them. After pausing for only a few moments, they were pushed forward onto the trail again.

Travel was even more fatiguing now with the heavy, wet clothes that clung and rubbed against their legs. Their soggy leather shoes slid and squeaked on their feet with each step they took. They journeyed on, generally following the course of the winding creek. The trail was wider now down in the open along the creek bed where game coming to feed and drink had trampled pathways. They continued on that course until just before dark when they veered off into the woods and came to what looked like an empty Indian camp. It was way back under the pine trees. Wooden stakes made of trimmed tree limbs had been driven into the ground on a slant for a roof. They had been covered with large strips of bark layered on them to make a covered lean-to. It was open all along the front of the structure. It appeared to have been used quite often since worn paths were heading from it in several directions.

Ina, with Christopher and Amelia, was shoved into the back corner of the lean-to. They quickly collapsed to the ground, totally exhausted; they had travelled over fifteen miles that day. They were scared and shaky as they huddled against each other and tried to get warm in their damp clothes. Nervously they watched to see what the Indians would do next. Constayunka started talking to Shomachsom and soon the smaller Indian came over to them and tossed them a small strip of dried venison. Ina had made dried venison from the deer Cornelius had shot and knew it was good nourishment. Right away Amelia chewed on it hungrily, and Ina cautioned her to slow down as best as she could in hoarse whispers and hand signals. Ina's jaw and mouth were so sore she couldn't chew and swallow food herself. She still had the taste of her own blood in her mouth from being struck. She broke off a small piece from her strip of venison with her fingers, held it in her painful mouth to soften and moisten it, and then put it into Christopher's mouth for him to eat. She motioned to Amelia to chew some first for Christopher too. She thought the Indians would let them rest in the back corner of the lean-to for the night, and even hoped one of them would start a fire. She wanted to get warm and have her children warm also, but soon Shomachsom came over and pulled her to her feet while she still held onto Christopher.

Amelia quickly tried to stand up with them too, but he pushed her back down and motioned her to stay there. Ina reached out to pull her close, but he forced Amelia to go back where she was in the lean-to. Amelia sat down in a back corner and hugged her knees, rocking back and forth as she saw the Indian lead her mother with her baby brother away. He took Ina about fifty feet from the lean-to and hacked some bushes away to clear a spot. Then he threw down a blanket and pushed Ina down onto it. He forced Ina to lay Christopher down. Then, Shomachsom took a limb the size of a broomstick and put it behind Ina's back. He bent her arms behind her and lashed them to the stick with twine. Now she couldn't move to take care of Christopher. Fortunately, he was so tired the little boy soon fell sound asleep, wrapped in his blanket lying against her side.

That was how Ina spent her first night in captivity. She sat in the dark and cold with her arms pinned behind her and her small sleeping child lying against her. Her clothes were still quite damp and cold from crossing the creek earlier. She had her baby, but she didn't know if her brave daughter was safe back in the lean-to alone with the Indians. She didn't know either what had happened to her husband earlier that morning. Had he come back and found them gone and the cabin ransacked by now? Was he trying to get a neighbor to help hunt for them? Or worse, was he dead? And her frail, little Rubin, had he really died? Had he suffered, or was it a sudden end? "Oh, my little Rubin . . . Why?" she asked the silent dark sky, sobbing. She shook her head; she couldn't think about him without becoming deeply distraught. Bitter, sad tears rolled unchecked down her cheeks.

She was alone now, except for her little baby who slept with her on that Indian's rough blanket in those strange, dark woods. She prayed Amelia was sleeping and all right and hoped her instincts about Constayunka protecting her daughter were right. She wanted to think about what to do, how to get them all out of this danger. She wanted to talk to Cornelius, but he wasn't there to help now. She raised her head up again to look at the stars through the canopy of the dark treetops and thought about how Cornelius always said they were shining down on their homestead too. She prayed to God for help and direction, but no peace or answers came. Finally, mercifully, her body and mind, not able to take any more, went to sleep and ended the aching in her body and soul until dawn.

CHAPTER 4

THE NEXT MORNING, SHE WOKE TO the song of birds after a fitful sleep of disturbing dreams. A white gauzy mist had risen from the creek and hung in the air around the camp. Constayunka came to where she was and untied her arms from the pole across her back. She flexed and stretched them to try to ease the aches and tightness of being tied like that for the night. Ina picked up Christopher, who was now awake, and carried him back to the lean-to camp. As soon as she saw Amelia, she anxiously asked her in a hoarse whisper if she was alright. Amelia had rested a little, she said, but she had been very cold because her clothes had not dried completely. Constayunka and Shomachsom hadn't started a campfire last night, but instead alternated watches at the lean-to.

Constayunka left them again to back track along the trail and see if they were being followed. Ina was talking quietly to Amelia in the lean-to and noticed Shomachsom had cut a whip-like willow branch and bent it into a hoop. He reached inside his tunic and pulled something out. Then he started stretching it onto the hoop. It wasn't until he turned it over that Ina saw the tangle of golden hair and recognized it as her son Rubin's. "Oh, my God . . . No," she tried to shout, but only choking noises came out. Then she immediately lunged at him with her arms flailing away. Shomachsom reached for his tomahawk and had his arm raised to strike a killing blow. Just in time, Constayunka returned and grabbed his wrist to protect Ina from the fatal strike.

Ina fell to her hands and knees and dug her fingers into the earth, sobbing loudly. Constayunka and Shomachsom started

34

arguing again and this time it was very heated and animated. They both pointed toward her and Amelia. During their arguing, Ina pulled herself together and decided that she had to control her hatred for now. She would plan her revenge on Shomachsom and at the first opportune moment, she would murder him. Then she would escape with her children. The two Indians came to some sort of settlement; the shouting stopped and they both calmed down. Constayunka pulled Ina forcefully to her feet and shoved her toward her children. She picked Christopher back up. The Indians herded the captives back together and everyone got back onto the trail and pushed forward again.

Ina ached all over, inside and out. She had spent such an uncomfortable night pinioned on the ground with her arms behind her. More than once she had tasted her own blood in her mouth, and today her face was swollen and bruised black and blue. She still couldn't move her mouth to speak clearly because it hurt far too much. She wanted to try to question Constayunka again in English. What did they plan, and where were they going? But she couldn't raise her voice above a hoarse whisper or even move her split, swollen lips to form coherent words.

The group traveled all day, barely stopping along the beaten path. In some areas it crossed a marsh full of sedge and saw grasses that scraped and cut their legs, and their pace was slowed down to negotiate the slippery dark mud. Ina's arms were numb from carrying the baby for so long and her lower back throbbed painfully. She set him down at every little pause they took because he also wanted to be out of her arms to move around. By dark they had again covered quite a distance. They stopped at a sheltered area back against a rock cliff to spend the night. She and Amelia were given another strip of dried venison to eat. It was their only meal of the day. Ina watched the two Indians enjoy some of the biscuits they had stolen from the cabin, but they didn't share them with their captives. It was anguishing to chew the venison, but she did, taking little pieces at a time, softening it, and then sharing it with Christopher.

In a short while she was again taken, still carrying Christopher, a distance away from Amelia and the camp. There her arms were pinioned behind her as before and she was left with Christopher on a blanket in the same manner as the night before. There was no fire to keep them warm. She did her best to keep him covered and sheltered from the night and the elements, but he was restless and uncomfortable too. She recited the simple child's prayer to him as best she could, "Now I lay me down to sleep . . ." She choked when she got to, "If I should die before I wake" and couldn't continue. At least her clothes had mostly dried that day. Soon Christopher fell asleep lying against her and she thanked God for the innocence of young children. She also prayed God would protect them all now. She dozed fitfully as she had done the night before. At one point in the night she dreamed she walked back into her cabin and saw a glowing fire in the fireplace and all her children playing in the big room. Cornelius sat there cleaning his gun. That was her last thoughts until she awoke again to the sound of birds singing in the forest.

Shomachsom came over, untied her arms, and pushed her back toward the others. Before long, the whole group was on the trail again. It had been over two days now and they had traveled about thirty-five miles walking since leaving the cabin back at the edge of the field. They had gone up and down mountainsides, across creeks, through marshes, and now along another narrow trail. She still wondered where they were going and what awaited her family when they got there. They veered off the trail toward a river and crossed the flat, wide riffles in the shallow water that ran over a bed of gravel. There was a small island across this stretch of water that the river split like a "Y" to run around it. They waded through shallow water to get to the island. Once there, Ina saw the Indians pull out two white birch bark canoes that were hidden in the brush. She realized the Indians must have left them there to be used after their raid. Perhaps they were now going to travel by canoe.

On the island, the men seemed to argue with each other over what to do. They continued to shift items back and forth between them, and then put their things into separate canoes and carried them down to the opposite shore of the island where the main current was. Decisions must have been made between them, and Shomachsom, the smaller Indian that Ina hated, came over, took Amelia, and put her into a canoe with him. Ina and Christopher were led to the other canoe with Constayunka. The water was murky, deeper and swifter on this other side of the island, and their Indian captors had to paddle hard against the current to go upstream. She could tell by the moss on the trees and the stars she had seen last night that they had been pushing northwards. Traveling by canoe was a mixed blessing for Ina. She was so exhausted from all the walking and carrying her baby it was good to be able to sit. She had the chance now to put Christopher down by seating him between her feet in the bottom of the canoe. Christopher seemed content with the new experience of riding in the canoe and the movement of it. She was sure Amelia needed to get off her feet too; her little legs must be even more tired. But she was with Shomachsom, that evil acting savage. Thank God Constayunka had power over Shomachsom, she thought, and felt Amelia was safer because of that.

Stress and exhaustion took control, and Ina found herself captured by the primal beauty of her surroundings. She looked around her as they traveled and saw the familiar velvet deep green of the Eastern pines and forest she loved so much. The canoes made very little noise as they moved through the water. They were so light and buoyant they seemed to just glide across the surface of the river. Ina saw sleek, golden brown deer come down to the water's edge to drink, then raise their heads and watch the canoes glide by as beads of water dripped from their muzzles. Constayunka's canoe, with Ina, led the way and Shomachsom followed in their wake. The Indians' steady pull of the paddles in the water made a rhythmic watery sound as they were plunged in and lifted back out with each stroke.

The sun made brilliant sunbursts bounce off the small wakes the paddles made each time they were moved, stroking the cold water. Ina looked into the water beside them and saw fish in her shadow that darted away from the canoe. The fish turned swiftly just underneath the surface and she could see their silvery-sided bodies flash below and then disappear out of sight. She saw a tall, wading grey-blue heron just ahead of them. He was alerted by the movement of the canoe and lifted his wide gray wings and started flying away. He moved as if in slow motion in front of the canoe and flew just a few feet over their heads. His knobby kneed legs trailed behind him like a kite tail. He lifted and dropped his wings in synchronism with the movement of the paddles as if leading them. Then he suddenly turned off to the left and flew out of sight.

They were still heading north and Ina looked behind the canoe she and Constayunka were in to see if Amelia was alright with Shomachsom. That's when she noticed his canoe had turned into the mouth of a deep creek that flowed into the river and the two parties were separating. It had never dawned on her that her captors might split up. She had just thought they were in two canoes because of the size of the party. Horrified, Ina tried to stand, but she sat back down quickly when the canoe rocked violently and nearly capsized them. Constayunka yelled at her to stay seated and Ina obeyed, realizing that Christopher could drown if she tipped the canoe over. Amelia waved frantically to Ina and called out, "Momma, Momma, Momma . . ." Ina still couldn't talk or shout well to her sweet daughter; her jaw was still too painful to move much. All she could do was wave slowly and sadly, and see her Amelia disappear out of sight. Tears flowed down her cheeks again and fell onto Christopher's head as another of her precious children left her life.

Ina watched Amelia leave in the canoe until it turned past a bend and there was no sign of her any longer. She then turned back around to face upstream toward her future. She pleaded silently to God to keep her Amelia safe and vowed someday, somehow, she would find her again, no matter what it took. Then she realized the further from the cabin she was being taken, the less her chances were of being able to get back home. She started to secretly plan her escape again as she sat there in the canoe with the big Lenape watching every move she made. "At least he cannot steal my thoughts," she told herself. "At least he cannot steal my thoughts."

Further up the river Constayunka paddled them into a deeper and wider stretch of river where it was easier going and he made better time moving the canoe forward. When they pulled into shore for the night, they were far from what she had known as her home. For the first time, she was not pinioned down for the night after she was given the dried venison to eat. She was able to sleep lying down, snuggling Christopher close to her. Constayunka was keeping a watch on her and the baby. He had saved her life twice when Shomachsom wanted to tomahawk her, but she felt no gratitude toward him. She still hated him for his part in the death of Rubin, the separation of her family, and the hardships they were now suffering. She studied the dark woods and prayed for Cornelius to be there somewhere with other men to save her, but it was still and silent.

Despite her upbringing as a Christian woman, she felt no forgiveness for these people who were so different from her and whom she now considered cruel and barbarous. Somehow, she was going to get away and try to save herself and Christopher. She realized she could never outrun this large, athletic man or subdue him in any way. She also realized she could not talk him into letting her go. There had to be some way she could slip away from him. It was her only possibility. She had to watch for an opportunity before they got to wherever he was taking them. Escape after that would be much harder, if not impossible, and she would be even further from home. *There would be many more Indians where we are going. I might even get tortured or separated from Christopher,* she thought. Constayunka must want to keep us alive for something. Then the thought came into her head, *oh, my God, what if I am to be his wife?* No, not ever, she couldn't think about that anymore. She wrapped her arms around Christopher, hiding him against her. She fell asleep with her mind still trying out and rejecting different ways to escape. Much later, she woke in the middle of the night because Christopher had been lying on her arm, and it throbbed from lack of circulation. She shifted him carefully and quietly and looked across the small encampment at Constayunka. He was sound asleep, taking slow deep breaths, interrupted occasionally by a loud snore. Suddenly, she realized this was the opportunity of escape she had been hoping for.

Christopher was sleeping soundly where she had laid him too, so she dragged herself cautiously toward Constayunka and the precious sack that held the dried venison. Hunger had already knawed at her stomach and she knew they must have some food or they'd never make it. She held her breath and painstakingly slid her hand into the deerskin sack. Ina watched Constayunka's face for any sign of movement all the while. She was so close she could smell the sweaty scent of his body and breath as he exhaled. She eased out what venison she could get her hands on in the sack without making any noise or alarming him. She already felt faint from lack of food. She reached into the sack again and her fingers touched the precious silver thimble that had been her mother's. A pang of remembrance made her flinch as she retrieved it and tucked it into her pocket along with the venison. Then very slowly, tediously, she inched her way backwards out of the camp and away from her captor, all the while keeping her eyes on the sleeping figure. She stood, gently picked sleeping Christopher up and held him close, turned, and quickly started walking away. She was apprehensive with every step that she might break a twig or branch and alert Constayunka or wake up Christopher by her movements. Fortunately, her steady walking lulled him back to a deep sleep, and once she felt she was clear of the camp, she picked up her pace.

Now she was not so worried about making too much noise, just concerned about getting as fast and far away as she could before Constayunka woke and discovered she was gone. She didn't know why he hadn't pinioned her arms that night. Perhaps he thought a woman with a small baby so far from home would never take off in the dark woods alone. Perhaps God gave her the help she had prayed for. Whatever the reason, she was grateful, yet terribly frightened. *But at least I have a chance to find my way home*, she thought. The adrenalin surging in her veins was quickening her steps and she stumbled a few times, then slowed down slightly. It would ruin everything to twist an ankle now. It was dark, but enough light from the stars and moon was shining through the trees that she could see to avoid obstacles. She headed straight for what she thought was the direction of her cabin along the path they had come from, using the stars again for navigation. Then it dawned on her that Constayunka would surely take this same route to catch up to her when he realized she was gone. So she changed her route in hope that it would still lead her home. *Please God, don't let Constayunka wake until morning*, she begged. She would stay off the trail they had been travelling on and make a big sweep around the last mountain they had crossed and then swing back toward the cabin. *That could deceive him, and he won't catch me*, she thought. It was risky; she could get really lost in this strange place. But it was even more risky to go back along the same way they had come on the Indian trail. She just hoped she had learned enough from Cornelius from their journey north to navigate by the stars and not get lost forever. She walked steadily on the rest of the night until she saw the darkness start to lift and the early dawn light the sky.

When the sun came up high enough, she paused and checked her direction against it, but then pressed on. She only stopped momentarily to adjust how she held Christopher, or to get a drink. She walked through tall briars that caught at her and scratched and gouged her skin and face. She went through thorn apple thickets that had lethal 3-4" wooden daggers on them that stabbed at her clothes, arms, and legs. It was so difficult going through them and protecting Christopher from being hurt. She held her cloak in her sore mouth to make a sling of fabric to shield him. She had to use her arm to push back the branches so they didn't swing back and lash at their faces, but the thorns pierced her sleeve and sunk into her flesh.

The pain in her jaw was still so intense it made her whole head hurt and shooting pain was running down the whole length of her spine with each step. The agony of trying to hold the cloak in her teeth to protect Christopher kept her senses on edge. By the time she worked her way through the thorns and back into another area of the woods, her arms, face, hands, and legs had deep scratches and punctures that were bloody rivulets. Broken thorns had stuck into her and the ends were sticking out from her flesh. Red streams of blood ran down her arms and legs and were smeared all over her skin by her moving clothes. But Ina couldn't stop to rest yet. She had to put distance between her and Constayunka; he could be just a few steps behind her. At sunset she traveled down a hill and ascertained where she was by the evening star just coming out. She hadn't stopped except for a few minutes all day, after sleeping for just a few hours in Constayunka's camp the night before. She had to rest now; she was too exhausted to go on.

Ina found a sheltered area back against some rocks. She gathered up a pile of dry leaves for a mattress with her hands and settled Christopher into their makeshift bed. She took out a hunk of the stolen dried venison, chewed what she could and noticed some of her teeth were loose from the cruel blow she had taken from Shomachsom. She shared the softened meat with her baby, the only family member she now had that she could touch and hold. He represented all of them to her now. She pulled out what embedded thorns she could before she fell into another uneasy sleep. The deep, broken off ones would have to stay in her flesh for a while, because she had nothing to dig them out with. She found some cool damp moss within reach and laid it on the most damaged, painful spots to try and soothe her wounds. Poking around in the leaves she found a small puffball and instantly thought of Amelia as her tears began to flow. Just a few days earlier she had taken one from her hand while gathering hickory nuts. It seemed like so long ago to her now. Ina used the brown powder to stop some of the blood that was still flowing from her wounds. Christopher had only a few minor scratches and she was at least thankful she had protected him from the thorns.

She knew she should stay awake and alert, but also realized she had to rest to keep going the next day. What would Constayunka do to them if he caught them? No, she couldn't think like that . . . *I will get back home,* she told herself. *I must keep my strength up. I must rest.* She tried to stay awake for a little while longer to see if her captor had been tracking them, but after Christopher started dozing soundly, she too fell asleep. If Constayunka walked into her little camp that night, he would find her snuggled tight in her leaf bed with Christopher under the moonlight, sound asleep. She was too tired to even think or dream of anything.

CHAPTER 5

CHRISTOPHER STARTED CRYING AND WOKE INA at the first light of morning when the birds started their morning song. She sat up with a sudden jerk, instantly realizing she shouldn't stay there any longer. She had slept during the night without waking for the first time since being captured. How many days was it now? Lack of real nourishment and fatigue was taking its toll. It was getting hard to think and she was starting to lose track of time. She couldn't let her mind wander to Rubin, Amelia, or even Cornelius. She had to concentrate on herself and saving little Christopher for now. She knew it was a miracle she had slipped away from Constayunka. But he could suddenly emerge from the woods any minute to recapture her. Other Indians could even find her since she was beyond the settler's frontier and following streams in her search for a way back.

She and Cornelius had traveled to their homestead on the Williamson Road along Larry's Creek. They had learned from others at the Blockhouse that when the Pennsylvania Authorities pushed the Indians further north, their well-traveled paths often became new roads for the pioneers. The Indians always used creeks and game trails to guide them to other places. In the wilderness they were natural landmarks they could always use to orient themselves. Ina knew if she stayed close to the creeks she could get back home, but she also took the chance of running into other Indians by doing that. So she stayed back further in the woods, but still skirted the course of the stream. "I must stay alert and on the move," she said aloud. She could talk a little better now, and as she walked, she quietly told Christopher stories and little rhymes she had also taught her other children. Now she was reciting "Jack and Jill went up the hill" to him.

Occasionally she'd come across some sort of berry she knew was okay to eat. The bright red, minty wintergreen berry grew on low plants and every so often she'd find a few ripe ones to pick. She chewed on them a little and shared with Christopher. Even the leaves tasted good to chew. It would get her hunger going though because it was such a tiny amount of food. There were other berries in the woods, but she knew some of them were deadly. She had come across some fat blue berries that looked edible and had almost tasted them before she saw a dead sparrow lying under the bush. It was too close a call, so she decided not to try anything else unless she knew exactly what it was, no matter how hungry they got.

Sometimes she'd find a feather to give Christopher to play with and it kept him occupied for a little while. He was holding a blue jay feather now and chattering "boo jay, boo jay." They traveled in that manner all day. Ina gave him something else when he lost interest in what he had, or he napped as she carried him.

After sunset, a light rain started to fall and Ina stopped for the night. Every time she sat Christopher down to gather up leaves for their bed, he started to cry. She feared they might be discovered by the noise he was making. She picked him up and soothed him again until he was quiet. Then Ina heard the sound of crunching twigs in the woods. Because the soil had been dampened from the rain, she was concerned that she could have left visible tracks. She looked around for a place to hide and saw a huge tree that had recently been blown down. It had a massive trunk, thick foliage, and lots of big branching limbs. She crept in among them with Christopher in her arms and lay low within the leaves and branches tight against the trunk. Peering through the leaves she saw an Indian moving stealthily towards them. He came over to where he thought he'd heard a sound. It wasn't Constayunka; it was a different Indian, perhaps a wandering hunter.

He had a gun, and close by Ina, he crouched down and looked around him. He was so near she could hear the sound of something he was wearing bump against the metal of his gun. Christopher became warm and comfortable against her and lay quiet while they hid there in very real danger. The Indian crouched in that unbroken silence for nearly an hour, listening intently. Ina's fear was so profound she was sure he could hear the noise of her pounding heart. She trembled in terror and thought she would break down from the agonizing stress. Finally, the flutelike sound of a night owl came from another part of the woods a distance away. The Indian jumped up and answered his companion with a horrid yell and departed. Ina was grateful she had thought of covering Christopher's ears, and thanked God her and her baby's life were spared again.

She crouched there and hid low among the branches and leaves of the fallen tree the rest of the night. She had noticed it was a giant hickory before she fell asleep and dreamed that night of being in her familiar area of the forest again with Amelia and Rubin gathering nuts. When she awoke in the morning, she heard birds and the chattering of two squirrels running on the broad limbs of the hickory tree. The fat one was chasing the other and caught up to it, sending it tumbling head over tail off the log and onto the ground. Then it pounced and bit it savagely. The smaller squirrel was visibly wounded and darted away, leaving a trail of blood. Ina shuddered at the sight. After the squirrels were both gone, she looked at the area around her in the morning light.

There were hickory nuts all around and she gathered as many as she could. The handfuls of nuts were bulging in her pockets as she set out again. She shifted Christopher into a comfortable carrying position. The scare with the Indian last night had made her extremely cautious today. She was afraid that she may walk into one of their lean-to camps or cross their trail while trying to get home. This was, after all, Indian country, their territory. She had to be constantly looking way ahead of her as well as behind her while still keeping the stream in her sight through the trees at the same time. Vigilance was important. Vigilance was life.

Ina passed through some stands of mountain laurel again. The thick bushes with their leathery green leaves and twisting branches were a tangled growth well over the height of her head. She had moved halfway up on a mountainside. Now the ravine where the creek ran was narrow and steep all the way down to the water. It was very hard to see any distance ahead of her while walking in the heavy cover. She was following some sort of game trail that skirted the side of the mountain but was away from the openness of the stream. She turned a corner and started down a gradual slope when something dark caught her eyes on the trail ahead. It was two black bear cubs rolling around and wrestling with each other. She stood and watched their comical antics and couldn't help but chuckle at how much they looked like little children who teased, poked, and chased each other in play. One cub would wrap its arm around the other's neck and chew on its ear. Then the victim would break away and circle around to jump on the back of its sibling. All thoughts left her mind for a few moments as she saw them play in their wild home. She had never been so close to animals like this before and was transfixed watching them. Then Christopher got restless, cried aloud, and suddenly both cubs stopped playing and looked towards her. When they saw her standing there, they became alarmed and separated. Each one ran up a separate tree by the path. Once in the trees they looked her way and then bawled loudly. It was a noise that sounded like a deep, "Maaww, maaww."

Suddenly Ina's fascination changed to terror as she heard bushes being crushed and branches snapping off to the right of the cubs. Quickly, with her heart racing and goose bumps raised on her skin, she stepped backwards on the trail and tried to hide. All the while she kept her eyes focused in the direction of the noise. She also put her hand over Christopher's mouth to silence him. Her legs were limp and she thought her knees would buckle with each step she took backward, but she was making progress distancing herself from sight and scent.

Ina didn't see the mother bear come crashing out of the laurel thicket to check on her bawling cubs, but she heard her growl to them in their trees and their bear cub noises back. Ina hid trembling beside the trail for most of the morning. She knew sow bears with cubs were extremely dangerous, and she couldn't backtrack too far on the steep hillside. She thought she had heard the mother bear and cubs move off but wasn't sure how far away they had gone. She was afraid to go forward in case the bear and her cubs were still close by and she'd run right into them again.

"Cornelius told me bears liked to bed down in laurel thickets," she said to herself. "Why didn't I remember that?" Probably that sow had been taking a short nap while the cubs played and was startled awake by their bawling. Finally, after hours of waiting, Ina summoned the courage to go ahead and quickly passed through that area safely. She had lost a lot of time that day and didn't progress much. Besides waiting for the bears to move off, she also had to go up and down the sides of ravines to follow the course of the creek and stay out of the open terrain. When she escaped from Constayunka and purposefully traveled away from the river to lose him, she had come across this stream. The water seemed to flow back in the right direction to swing around to the river that should take her back home. But what if she were wrong? What if the elevation of this stream came off a terrain so high it ran southwest instead of southeast and she was actually going deeper into the interior? Ina checked her course against the sun and hoped she was right. She was staking both their lives on it.

When evening came, she raked leaves together with her hands for their bed again. A lot more leaves had drifted down from the trees in the last few days. She shared the final piece of dried venison she had stolen with Christopher. She could already see he had lost some weight and knew by the way her clothes were fitting she had too. She broke up the hickory nuts as quietly as she could by hitting them with a rock on a fallen log and picked each precious piece of nutmeat out with a sharp stick. For her and Christopher it was a real treat. They had come across several springs while walking and water was not a problem, but food was so scarce for them that anything, even these small morsels, seemed like a banquet.

There was an icy damp chill in the air this night and she huddled tight with Christopher against another fallen log large enough to be like a low wall behind them. Already the gathered leaves were not keeping them warm enough, so she broke off some low hemlock branches and used the soft green pine boughs as a coverlet over them. Christopher started to cough and sounded congested. "Tomorrow I'll look for some wild mint to help you with that cough," she said to him. She wanted so much to have a fire, but the danger of being caught was very real. Besides, she doubted she could ever rub sticks together hard enough to make kindling smoke and flare as she had seen others do. She fell asleep and dreamed of the warm cabin and its glowing fireplace again. In the middle of the night, she suddenly woke to the loud sound of an animal killing some prey nearby. She heard the rustle of dry leaves during the chase and then a high-pitched animal scream that suddenly cut off. It was the horrible, terrified scream of some small animal that knew its end was coming and then no noise at all. A weighty silence filled the darkness, and then it was perforated by the victory growl of a mountain lion.

She held onto Christopher tightly and shielded him with her cloak. Then she reached around in the dark for a strong stick, broke the end into a jagged point. and stayed there, half lying, half sitting, against the log. She held the pointed stick like a crude spear for protection. Sleep was impossible now, only dozing and waking for the rest of that cold night. She had never felt like prey before, but now she knew she was. Prey for the Indians, who were probably still looking for her, and prey for the wild animals roaming in the woods. She was prey for injury and sickness here. She was prey, too, for starvation, which seemed to be stalking her. Ina had never felt more alone in the gripping desolation of the dark and danger-ous forest.

When morning came, she and Christopher again headed out. She saw the signs of the mountain lion kill the night before. It wasn't far from where she had tried to sleep. Ferns and leaves were all ripped up and there were bits of torn out rabbit fur scattered around. There were also places where the big cat had skidded to a stop in the chase, and his feet had dug deep into the soft ground. There was no mistake; it had been a mountain lion. The paw prints were huge with deep claw ditches gouged in the earth.

Ina hurried to get out into the more open area of the creek, look-ing around nervously as she did. When she left the forest margin, she saw that the damp, bitter cold of the night before had been caused by a frost. She could see her breath and the weeds had a white coating of ice crystals. For the first time, she felt she really might die alone in the wilds of Pennsylvania. If she didn't find her way home before winter, they would starve or become prey for one of those roaming animals in the night. If she died of exposure or fatigue, what would become of Christopher?

With bone chilling horror, she realized that if she got so bad she couldn't go on anymore, she would have to put Christopher to sleep forever. She decided she would suffocate him, if she had to, rather than let him starve or be attacked by animals. She discovered a part of herself she never knew existed, a part she loathed. A part that could make her do a horrible thing to her child. It deeply, deeply saddened her to know that she had that capability in her soul to kill this beautiful child and would use it as a last resort. Shocked to discover such a despicable part of herself, she became nauseous, turned her head away from Christopher, and retched.

How had her life come to this? They had been so happy in their cabin with so many plans for the future. Now she didn't even know who was left in her family or if she'd ever see her home again. She kissed the top of Christopher's head as she carried him. Ina could no longer cry, she was too tired even for tears. *No, I can't let that happen to Christopher,* she vowed. *I will survive; I will get back home to Cornelius if he's still alive, somehow. I will get back home,* she reassured herself.

She checked her direction by the sun that was starting to burn off the frost and decided to risk walking by the stream for a short while. She wanted to find some mint or other herb for Christopher's cough. It might help him, and mint usually grew close to water. It was easier terrain to walk today and they covered more ground. After it warmed more, it turned into a beautiful fall day. She looked at her surroundings and again noticed how pristine and beautiful this frontier country was.

The small, round leaves of the white birch tree were colored butter-yellow now and twisted and flashed in the sun when the wind blew them even slightly. The stark white bark with its black flecks on its trunk was almost blinding if the sun hit it just right. The clustered white tree trunks stood out against the deep, forest green boughs of the pines, and those Eastern pine trees were so tall and massive. They looked old and wise towering over many of the other trees in the forest. A layer of brown burnt sienna pine needles lay all around their bases like a carpet. The oaks had changed colors too. Some were bronze now, or copper and brown colored. The sugar maples were the most brilliant trees with full, bright red tresses of leaves that swayed in the breeze.

A small flock of geese were stitching their "V" formation across the sky as they left the colder climes for warmer surroundings before it was too late. Ina listened to their honking that kept getting further and further away, wishing she could be up there with them to look for her home.

CHAPTER 6

THE BLUE SKY OVER THE STREAM was brilliant, and the warming sun felt so good on her tired, aching body. She was surrounded by the splendor of nature and it lifted her spirits some. She walked along the water and came across a bunch of wild peppermint that grew at the creek's edge and pulled some out to give to Christopher. She sat him on a big warm rock and told him to chew on some of the tender leaves; maybe the juice would soothe his throat. When she pulled the mint out at the edge of the water, she noticed some small, silver fish darting away. She carefully picked up some submerged rocks to try and catch a fish that might be hiding underneath. No matter how carefully she lifted the rock or how fast she grabbed, they always darted away and left a cloud of muddy water behind.

They were just little fish, only a few inches long, but they could be food, something to keep them alive. She was desperate enough to eat them raw if she could just catch them. Christopher needed the nourishment, she thought as she looked back at him sitting on the rock. They both had to survive. She kept trying to catch the darting fish. She placed her cupped hand so they had to swim into it when she lifted a rock but she couldn't close her fingers fast enough to grab one. Disgusted, she slammed the rock into the water, hitting another rock. She splashed herself and Christopher laughed at her. She was ready to turn away and give up when she noticed a couple fish floated to the surface. She had stunned them with the percussion of the two colliding rocks. Quickly she reached down and grabbed them, put them into her pocket, and hit another rock under the water. More stunned fish floated up, which she grabbed before the current took them away or they revived. She didn't have many fish when she quit, but she had enough for her and Christopher to have a little meal.

Then Ina realized she had forgotten caution and had made a lot of noise down by the creek. A bird flew up and she stood still, frozen, alert. She turned, looked up and down the stream, and scanned the forest for any movement. She quickly decided they had better move back into the dark edge of the forest and went to get Christopher, who had wandered off his rock. As she did that, she noticed the recent track of an Indian moccasin in the soft mud and became doubly alert. How long ago was the track made? She had the feeling again that she and Christopher were prey and would be until they got back home. She quickly scooped him up and stepped back into the shelter of the pine trees and the dense woods that surrounded the creek.

They ate better that day. Later she took the small fish out of her pocket. They were partially dried up and were so small there were no real bones to worry about. Once she got over the initial gagging of the first bites, they even tasted good to her. She chewed some and then gave the chewed meat to Christopher, who didn't seem to mind the taste of the new food. Besides the fish, she also came across some fox grapes on vines hanging from a tree. They were small, sort of bitter and astringent, but food that she knew was safe. She had kept some of the mint she found to nibble on. She also found some beech nuts and felt better about being able to gather some sort of food for a short while at least to keep them alive.

The territory opened more. The valleys were got wider and the hills were more rounded. *I must be getting closer to the river plain,* she said to herself. *I must be somewhere near home by now.* Questions flooded her thoughts again. *Did I get turned around in the woods when I couldn't see the sky? How much did I wander, I don't know? How much time did I lose going up and down the hillsides instead of moving forward? Is Constayunka just behind me ready to grab us both any minute? Are there other, more dangerous Indians or animals nearby?* All these things were going through her mind as she walked along. Hours and days and distances were all getting confused because she was so weary. Her clothes were covered with dirt and burrs and were uncomfortable. Her and Christopher's legs were raw from their unchanged undergarments even though she kept layering them with soft, dry moss.

She wanted a bath, to wash her matted hair and clean her baby up so his nose was shiny and his cheeks glowed and they both smelled good again. She had burrs stuck all over her, her nails were broken and dirty, and almost every inch of exposed skin was scratched, bitten by insects, bloody, or bruised. They stopped for a short rest that afternoon in a clearing. It was an area of large, flat, rectangular gray boulders and green ferns. Some of the large boulders were stacked or leaning on others like children's blocks. The treetops were closed in a leafy ceiling over their heads. She sat Christopher down so he could move around a little. Her arms ached from constantly carrying him. Then Ina had the idea of tearing off a wide part along the hem of her muslin nightgown to make a sort of sling to carry Christopher in. It worked when she tried it, and she cursed herself for not thinking of it before. Now, she had two arms free; even though it was going to put a strain on her neck and shoulders, she could now reach out and move branches out of the way and steady herself better while carrying him.

So far it hadn't been a bad day. They had eaten and made good forward progress. They were up and off again, trying to cover more ground before dark. *Let each step bring us closer to home, closer to Cornelius,* she prayed. Ina was going down a path that led next to some rocky outcroppings that were a cliff wall higher than her head. Lush, green ferns hung off ledges above her and loose shale had fallen from them and settled onto the path. It was rutted underfoot and hard going. Ina reached out and steadied herself on a rock that was jutting out from the cliff wall.

The movement of the snake's tongue flitting in and out got her attention before she heard the warning rattle. Her whole body slammed into place with the kind of joint locking jerk. The large, flat, triangular head of the snake rose above the wide coils of its body and pointed, swaying with its yellow eyes straight at her. Any sudden movement from Ina would make the snake strike her, so she kept her hand right where it was and fought the strong urge to pull it away. She stood there frozen on the outside but volcanic on the inside. Blood surged through her veins and every instinct said "run! run!" yet she remained statue-like. Finally, the snake settled down and with a slow, hesitant crawl it moved away, flicking its dark tongue in and out and unraveling its fat coils as it went.

As soon as it was safe to move her hand, she pulled it back, held Christopher tight to her, and started to run. She wanted to be out of the woods, away from bears, mountain lions, snakes, and most of all, murderous Indians. She ran the fastest she had ever run. She ran with no thought of going anyplace except out of there, away from there, as far and as fast as she could. She ran as if all the wolves of all the woods, large and small, were biting at her heels. She held Christopher tight to her chest as branches whipped and stung her face and sharp twigs reached out and tore at her legs. Roots humped up and tried to trip her. Trees moved and blocked her way and yet she dodged them. Her hair got snagged on a limb and she kept on running, tearing some of it out and leaving it behind like tinsel on a branch. She was driven forward by fear, desperation, and the need to be somewhere else but in those woods.

Ina broke out of the trees and into an open field. Still running, she stepped into a woodchuck hole and twisted her ankle. She flew forward, slamming her body hard to the ground. Christopher, luckily, had been somewhat protected by the sling, even though it tore, and she hadn't fallen on top of him. It had knocked the wind out of her but had also brought her back to her senses. Then she heard Christopher scream as he lay on the ground and reached out to pull him toward her. "Oh Christopher, baby, Momma's so sorry," she said as she checked him all over. He was all right, just scared, and his crying quieted as she soothed and kissed his forehead and cheeks and held him close to her. The crude sling she made had kept him from being flung hard to the ground. He only looked questioningly at her and gave out some shuddering sobs that shook his whole body now and then.

She sat at the edge of the field and rocked him gently back and forth. She ceased her comfort when she thought she heard a familiar noise. Ina listened intently. The wind was blowing the tall grass, making a low whishing sound. The leaves were rustling in the trees, and she could hear a blue jay squawking back in the depths of the woods. Then, faintly, in the wind, there it was again, a sound like a cow bell. She was sure it was a cowbell! She pushed her way to a standing position, shielded her eyes with her hand, and looked. She was standing at the top of an open hillside that led down to a river plain and a wide valley. Just across the river she saw two men working a field with horses and a couple of cows were grazing. She wanted to shout, to run, to hold Christopher over her head and spin around with joy. But her ankle hurt along with everything else on her body and her painful jaw still wouldn't allow her to call out loudly. So she carried Christopher and limped along slowly, but deliberately, down the field and onto the flat by the river toward the working men.

It wasn't hard to get their attention. Anyone working fields away from the settlements were constantly watching the forest edge. These farmers had heard of some recent raids in their area and were particularly vigilant. At first, they were very suspicious of her being alone. They shouted over, "Who are you?" Ina did the best she could to answer back that she had been captured by Indians, from Queen Esther's Flats. They told her to walk back and forth along the riverbank for a while to make sure she wasn't a decoy being used by the Indians to get more captives or scalps. Finally, one of the farmers got a boat that was tied nearby and came across to get her while the other one kept a flintlock to his shoulder aimed and ready. Ina almost collapsed into the farmer's arms when he finally reached out to help her and Christopher into the wooden boat. When she got to the other shore, they unhitched a workhorse and put her on its broad back. Then one farmer led it and the other farmer convinced Ina to let him take Christopher on his horse with him. For the first time in many days she was able to trust handing her baby over to someone else for a while.

They rode into a small settlement of about a dozen cabins. Ina was taken to the home of one of the village elders, the Clearys, and put onto a large feather bed. News soon spread throughout the settlement and men and women, along with their children, kept coming in and out of the cabin, asking her over and over again what had happened. They brought food and clothes with them for her and Christopher. The Clearys had several large dogs inside that barked continuously with each new visitor. Mrs. Cleary chattered away non-stop and was cooking some meat on the woodstove, loudly clanging pans and all the while shouting, "Praise the Lord, Praise the Lord for saving you!"

The smoky smell of the fire, the scent of meat that was being cooked, all the noise, the prying strangers, and the barking dogs were overwhelming. When Mrs. Cleary tried to force Ina to eat some food, all she could do was become nauseous and spit-up what little nourishment she had in her body. But Mrs. Cleary continued to fuss away at Ina, still trying to force her to eat some meat. She kept pushing a spoon at Ina's mouth saying, "You must eat something dear . . . You must eat something . . . Just try!" Christopher kept crying and was unhappy at all the strangeness and noise of the big dogs and people around him.

One of the visitors who came to see the woman who walked out of the wilds was an elderly lady named Mrs. Kenhart. She told the Clearys that all that commotion and attention wasn't good for Ina or the baby. Ina needed to go someplace more quiet and secluded. Mrs. Kenhart had helped most of them regain their health when they had been sick at one time or another and they respected her advice. Reluctantly the Clearys helped move Ina and Christopher to Mrs. Kenhart's quiet home where she was living alone. There, Ina was allowed to rest as long as she wanted, and nothing was forced on her. When she woke, Mrs. Kenhart was rocking a clean and happy Christopher by the fireplace. Mrs. Kenhart noticed Ina was awake and put Christopher down to play on the plank floor. Then she came over and held Ina's hands and looked at her tenderly.

Ina felt she could trust Mrs. Kenhart. She needed to talk about what had happened to her. Ina poured out the whole horrible story without stopping. She started from the beginning, telling of being dragged from her bed all the way to her walk down the field by the river's edge where the farmers were. Mrs. Kenhart held her hand and wiped Ina's face as tears streamed down her cheeks again. All the emotions she had been containing were finally turned loose. Ina had known as she looked into those kind elderly eyes that she could tell Mrs. Kenhart anything and she would understand and know the mother's pain in her soul.

When Ina finished talking, Mrs. Kenhart wiped away her own tears and tenderly washed Ina as if she were her baby. Then she helped Ina change into clean clothing. She gently and patiently brushed out Ina's tangled mass of hair and pinned it back for her. Most of the woody thorns imbedded in Ina's legs and arms had festered and Mrs. Kenhart carefully cleaned out the broken splinters and dressed the wounds with some wild herbal salve and bandages. She had no questions for Ina except, "What can I do for you?" When she was done ministering to her patient, she put a clean Christopher up on the bed with his mother and left them alone. She told Ina some men had gone to fetch her husband who was a full day away to the north. Ina had circled around in the woods as she planned but came out further down the river than she thought. But at least she was back with her own people.

Later that evening, Mrs. Kenhart offered her some thin broth and she was able to keep it down. When curious people came to the door with questions and prying eyes, Mrs. Kenhart firmly sent them away. The next day Ina felt well enough to stand for a while although her twisted ankle was swollen and painful. Her jaw and mouth were still hurting but steadily getting better. Christopher got along just fine with Mrs. Kenhart, who was a treasure. She made Ina thin potato soup that tasted warm and wonderful in her stomach. Christopher was not having any trouble eating and managed to have some of the soup and baking soda biscuits also.

That evening, after Christopher went to sleep beside Ina, all was still in the cabin except the fire crackling now and then and the gentle voice of Mrs. Kenhart reading her bible to Ina. When they were both ready to go to sleep for the night, Mrs. Kenhart got up from her rocker to snuff out the candles, but then they heard the sound of horses and a sharp knock at the door. Ina's heart leapt when the door opened. It was Cornelius who rushed in! He saw Ina and went right to her side. He reached out his arms and hugged her tightly to him. Finally, Ina could bury her face against the safety of her husband's chest and feel his strong, protective arms around her. She tried to speak, to tell him about the loss of their sweet Rubin, and how she had waved farewell to Amelia. But the words came out as choking, grief filled, and unintelligible sobs. "Shh . . .shh . . ." He said to her, kissing her eyelids, her hair, her scratched and bruised face. "Shh . . . tomorrow we'll talk, tomorrow is soon enough Ina." They sat there for a long time, holding each other, lost in their own thoughts. She fell asleep that way, safe in his arms. Cornelius wanted to know about Rubin and Amelia, but he knew he should not press Ina to tell him right then. The next day she recited her whole ordeal again. Mrs. Kenhart said sometimes the Indians sell their white hostages back and there was some hope of seeing Amelia again. Ina made Cornelius swear, as she had done while travelling in the canoe with Constayunka and the parties split, that someday they would find Amelia, no matter how long it took or how far they had to travel. Someday they would see their Amelia again.

CHAPTER 7

AMELIA'S JOURNEY

MELIA LOOKED AROUND ANXIOUSLY AS SHE sat in the front of Shomachsom's birch bark canoe. She, like her mother, had wanted to jump out of the canoe and swim away when the two canoes went in different directions. She thought of it now, but even young as she was, she knew if she tried to jump from the canoe, her clothes would get wet and heavier, making it impossible to swim. She was so afraid and shivered as she sat there because of the sudden separation from her mother and the unknown of the future. Shomachsom sat behind her in back of the canoe and steadily paddled up the deep creek that wound snake-like through the valley. Amelia thought of what had happened after they had been taken and followed a trail in the woods. She hadn't actually seen this Indian kill her brother. After Rubin fell over the ledge and her mother collapsed from being struck, Shomachsom disappeared down over the rocks for a while. When he returned without Rubin, Amelia was sure she saw blood on his hands. Her instincts told her Rubin was dead. She hated and feared this Indian who was now taking her away from her mother, father, and home.

Amelia could sense the Indian staring at her back, so she kept her body facing forward. She didn't want to turn and look at his frightening, unfamiliar face. What was going to happen next and where they were heading, she didn't know. She couldn't even plead with this man to let her go because he spoke no English. And what would she do if she could run away in this vast strange land? A wild animal could get her. How would she get back home to her father? She was so scared. They traveled in the canoe in a westerly direction, and she tried to pay attention to the scenery around her. They paddled in silence for a while. Occasionally, Shomachsom would hear a bird call out and he would cup his hand at his mouth and imitate the sound of its call. It amazed Amelia at how close his imitation was to the real birdcall. He even imitated the solitary high pitched "eee . . . eee" of a fish hawk that circled high above them. Often, he would call out his copycat birdcall and the birds would answer him back. Then they would fly in closer to see the new bird entering their territory, only to find out it was an imposter. Amelia's mind wandered from what was really happening and became totally absorbed with the birdcalls he was making. She wanted to learn how to talk to the wild birds like that and started silently mouthing the sounds when she heard Shomachsom make them.

There was little else for her to do besides worry and watch and silently pray as they traveled westward. Every so often they'd see a muskrat's house. Its dome shape was made of piled up brown grass, mud, and reeds. They saw the large rodent swimming about with his head up and a mouthful of grass held in his teeth. He looked like a small beaver only with a thin tail plowing water and sending out widening diagonal lines of wake from both sides of his body. The muskrats they saw were off to the side of the creek in a spread out marshy area and didn't seem to be disturbed too much by the canoe passing by in the main stream. Shomachsom even spoke to the muskrats as if he were talking to a friend or a brother, calling out, "Hè tëmàskwës." Though she couldn't understand his words, Amelia did notice the friendly tone of his voice when he called to them.

Amelia hadn't traveled anyplace by canoe before, and certainly not one made of thin layers of birch tree bark. She was fascinated by the things she saw along the waterway. Noisy redwing blackbirds flew up from the nests they'd made in swaying green cattails at the water's edge. Small brown turtles sunned themselves on partly submerged logs or slipped off them, splashing into the water as they passed by. Silvery fish rose to eat lacewing bugs just hatching from the water's surface and gulped them hungrily into their mouths before they had a chance to take their first flight. The fish made a boisterous jumping splash and left rings of ever widening circles behind as they dove back beneath the water to swallow their winged morsel. Amelia hung her hand over the side of the canoe and let her fingertips skim the top of the cold water. She wanted to connect with that strange, mysterious watery world of nature underneath the canoe.

The sun was low now in the west, and the bow of the canoe pointed right toward it. The mountains rose much higher around them in this area, with steep wooded sides. The white pine trees were so close together and thickly foliated it was impossible to see into the depths of the woods. Ahead of them, seven or eight deer had waded knee high into the water and were drinking its cool freshness. They raised their brown heads, twitched their ears forward and back and then, startled by the canoe's movement, they quickly turned and bounded away. Their white tails bobbed and waved goodbye to the canoeists as they disappeared into the tall grasses.

Shomachsom paddled the canoe on past that spot and pulled into shore. Then he jumped out and pulled the bow of the canoe out of the water to beach it. Amelia stepped out of the canoe and stood watching the Indian. He started gathering some kindling of dry grasses and wood for a fire. Then he took what looked like a small bow out of a leather bag he carried. It had a short round stick with it and a flat piece of wood with burnt, black circular depressions. Amelia carefully watched his every move. Shomachsom went away from the creek toward the wood's edge and squatted down with the little bow in his hands. He made a small pile of the dry grass. Then he stood the straight stick up in one of the depressions in the flat wood and used the bow with its sinew string to twirl the stick fast. It made hot friction at the base. As he did that, he blew into the small bunch of dry grass and eventually it smoked, then burst into flames, lighting up his frightening face.

It was getting dark. Shomachsom touched the burning bunch of grass to a larger bunch he had stacked with some small twigs on top of it. Then he painstakingly fed the fire with twigs and chunks of dry wood one at a time, blowing gently on it until he had a nice campfire going. Amelia was drawn like a moth to the first heat she'd felt in days and cautiously edged over by it to warm herself. The Indian reached into his pouch when he saw her come closer and pulled out more of the dried venison. He held it out to her, motioning for her to take it. She stretched her hand forward, being careful not to let her fingers touch his. She was sick of eating the same dried meat for days now but was very hungry at the same time. She was also smart enough to know nothing else was going to be offered. Shomachsom settled onto the ground by the fire and ate with gusto. He ripped and chewed off large bites of the tough dry meat like a ravenous animal. Amelia remained standing and slowly ate her share of the gamey jerky. The fire felt so good, and the light of it was comforting in the impenetrable dark that now surrounded them.

So far during the capture Amelia hadn't been pinioned down at all like her mother. She wondered if tonight she would have to suffer that ordeal. Instead, to her surprise, Shomachsom threw his only blanket down by the fire and motioned for her to get on it. Amelia was afraid of angering him. She hesitated, but then he forced her to sit down. Shomachsom then moved to a grassy spot across the campfire and lay down on the ground. He didn't pay any attention to Amelia; instead, he curled up and seemed to go to sleep.

Amelia sat looking into the fire for a long while and listened to the sounds of the creek flowing past their camping spot. The moonlight was hitting the ripples in the water and it looked like a silver shimmering road winding out of sight into the dark. She heard the deep flutelike "whoo . . . whoo" of an owl in the trees somewhere behind her. Then another softer call of a distant owl answered back from far away beyond the curtain of night. The dark silhouette of some small animal was moving around down by the stream's edge and Amelia guessed it was a raccoon hunting for crayfish. She sat there staring at the dancing light of the dying campfire flames a long time. She was terribly frightened and so alone. Her thoughts were of her safe bed back home and her family. When she was sure Shomachsom was sound asleep, she finally lay down and curled up in a fetus-like position. Much later, Amelia dreamed that she saw her father's smiling face and smelled the tobacco scent of his clothes. She slipped her hand into his big man's paw and wouldn't let it go.

When morning came, the movements of Shomachsom woke Amelia. He was gathering his belongings and getting ready to get back into the canoe. Amelia took the opportunity to quickly step behind some bushes to relieve herself. She didn't know how long she would be riding in the canoe again today. She really hated having to go to the bathroom with Shomachsom so close by. She felt so uncomfortable and vulnerable exposed that way, but she had no other choice. When she came back to the creek, Shomachsom was by the canoe and he gestured for her to immediately get in. He reached out his hand, but she ignored it. She would rather fall into the cold water than touch the hand of that savage. They were soon on their way heading northwest on Sugar Creek again.

Shomachsom and Amelia traveled many miles before he again pulled the canoe into shore. They got out and Shomachsom gave Amelia some things to carry. Then he hefted the birch bark canoe upside down over his head. He balanced it, and then struck out on a portage across land. The path they were traveling was worn down, as if it had been used many times by travelers. The portage wasn't far to the next stream and Shomachsom soon had the canoe back into the water. Amelia and he were moving westward once again. This stream had vast cattail and willow marshes spreading out from it in all directions. There were a lot of waterfowl along this waterway that quacked alarms at them and swam in nervous circles as they glided by. They saw beautiful wood ducks with colorful markings of white, blue, and bronze feathers. She chuckled when she saw mallard ducks stick their heads under the water and kick their webbed feet in the air as they fed on plants and bugs beneath the surface.

Further along, Amelia jumped when she saw the head and part of the body of a big black water snake swimming around. But when it went below the surface and came up again, she was surprised to see it was really a black duck with a fish in its beak and not a snake. Each new turn of the waterway brought new sights and wonders for Amelia. She had no idea of where they were going but was sure Shomachsom had been this way before. Eventually they glided around a sharp bend in the mud-banked stream and Amelia was alarmed because she could see an Indian village ahead of them. She learned it was The Great Meadows, a Lenape village in a large open meadow next to where Marsh Creek met the River of

Pines. This was a place where Amelia's life would change in ways she could have never imagined.

Shomachsom slowed the canoe by holding his paddle straight down in the water and turned it into the shore where other canoes were lying on the bank. Some Indians ran down to the water's edge to stare at the strange white girl and welcome Shomachsom back. He seemed to be an important man to many of them as they waved and greeted him. Shomachsom beached the canoe and got out. Amelia began shaking in terror again, not knowing what was going to happen. Some of them pulled her out of the canoe and pushed her forward toward the encampment of buildings. More Indians came out to see both of them as they got closer to the dwellings. Before long, children, barking dogs, and adults created quite a commotion at their arrival.

The dwellings that Amelia saw looked like some sort of wooden cabin from a distance. When Amelia got closer, she could see that they were shaped like a long bark covered house with a domed roof. There were places near the long houses where poles had been driven into the ground. Then another long pole was resting crossway between the uprights and tied bunches of husked ears of corn hung down from it. Children dressed in soft leather skins chased each other playfully, and then seeing Amelia, covered their mouths and laughed. They pointed their fingers at Amelia in her dirty, ragged clothes and disheveled appearance. These children with their dark shining hair and amber brown skin looked so healthy and neat compared to her. Amelia hadn't been able to comb her hair in days and was still in her bedclothes and cloak from the morning she was taken from her cabin. She was covered with mud and debris from walking and sleeping on the dirty trails of the woods and crossing the water. She tried to pull away when Shomachsom grabbed her by the arm and led her to the door of a longhouse. He and the rest of the crowd halted in front of it. He stood there and called out, "Mahonoy . . . Mahonoy." Soon a short, middle aged Indian woman pushed back the deer skin doorway and looked out at the gathering in front of the longhouse.

At first, she looked puzzled. Then, recognizing Shomachsom, she smiled and came forward to greet him. All those gathered there listened in hushed silence as Shomachsom greeted her. He pushed

Amelia forward toward Mahonoy and repeated, "Tòna . . . tòna." to her. Shomachsom told his Aunt Mahonoy that he had brought her a new daughter, Tòna, to take the place of the daughter the Great Spirit had taken from her. He said Amelia was the daughter of a strong white woman and had shown courage and strength in their travel there. She was proud also and had not shed many tears. He said she would serve Mahonoy well and take away the loneliness in her longhouse.

Mahonoy stepped over to where Amelia was and looked close into her face. She took hold of Amelia's chin and turned her head from side to side. Then she felt her shoulders and arms for muscles. Mahonoy walked around Amelia and lifted her right arm, then her left, and let them fall back to her side. She said something to the Indians watching her inspection that made them laugh. She held open Amelia's cloak and looked at her nightgown-covered body and shook her head as if she were seeing something pitiful. Mahonoy thanked Shomachsom, took Amelia's trembling hand, and led her through the deerskin door and into her longhouse.

CHAPTER 8

THE INSIDE OF THE LONGHOUSE WAS dark and smelled smoky. It was lit only by the light which came through an opening in the roof and the glow of a cooking fire on the ground. It took a few minutes for Amelia's eyes to get adjusted to the darkness. The framework of the bark-covered longhouse could be seen inside. It was made of young sapling poles, bent over and lashed together in large crisscrosses of sinew and handmade twine. There was a row of low bench-like beds along both sides just past the open cooking area. Above that row, higher up the wall, was another row of sapling bench beds. There were a lot of animal skins, baskets, bows, and quivers hanging on the walls. Indian clothing hung there too. The place where Amelia and Mahonoy were standing seemed to be only one section of the dwelling. Past the bench beds it looked as if there were a partition with another sort of animal skin doorway to another section of the longhouse. In the middle of this open kitchen section was a cooking fire with a few metal pans, pottery, gourds, plus cooking utensils on mats. Up over the fire area was a square hole in the bark roof for the smoke from the fire to escape through. A long pole was attached to a flap that opened or covered the hole as needed.

Mahonoy had some sort of food cooking in a pot that was suspended on a tripod over a fire that had burned down to glowing embers. The smell of the food stirred the gnawing hunger Amelia had been trying to ignore. There were mats made from dried and woven corn husks on the earth floor and Mahonoy led Amelia over to one and pushed on her shoulders, forcing her to sit down. Meanwhile, she was talking to Amelia in her Indian tongue as if she understood everything that was being said to her. Amelia had no idea of what she was saying but could tell by the emotion in the woman's voice that she was talking about something that caused her great sorrow. Amelia listened to the words of Mahonoy's story trying desperately to understand their meaning.

Mahonoy spoke of her "nichan," her daughter who had brought her great joy. Her little girl and only child, Kuskusky, had beautiful long, shiny black hair. She wore it in braids that hung down her back. She worked beside Mahonoy tending the three sisters they planted each year: corn, squash, and beans. The songs Kuskusky sang as they worked cheered Mahonoy's heart. When Kuskusky left her mother's side to play with the other Indian children, she always returned bringing her mother some flowers from the field, a rock that sparkled in the sun, or a pretty bird feather. Kuskusky would hide it behind her back and tease her mother to guess which hand she was hiding something in. Then after the game, whether Mahonoy guessed right or not, Kuskusky would give her the present and kiss her on the cheek. Then Kuskusky would run back outside the longhouse to stay in the sun and fresh air as much as she could before darkness fell.

Kuskusky had always been a happy, active child until one morning she woke with a fire in her body and a pain in her right side that made her roll back and forth in agony. Mahonoy brewed her herbs to soothe the fire and said prayers to the Great Spirit, but Kuskusky kept getting worse. Soon her beautiful daughter, who had sung songs of the cool gentle rains and earth flowers, had a raging fever and was moaning in constant pain. Mahonoy's hands could feel the hotness of the fire in her body. The medicine man was summoned and came with his wooden spirit mask carved from a live tree. He used a sacred turtle rattle and the smoke of some powerful plants to try and cleanse Kuskusky of the evil sickness. All Mahonoy could do was watch the medicine man circle her suffering daughter and call to the spirits for help as she lay suffering.

Kuskusky lay motionless and silent on the mat after a while. She looked so peaceful and quiet, as if she were sleeping. Mahonoy knew she was gone when she saw the eagle feather fall off the medicine man's headdress and hit the floor. It was a sign that the Great

Spirit had sent a sacred bird to come and carry Kuskusky's spirit away to another place. Mahonoy's husband had been summoned back from a hunting trip, but only the men sent to retrieve him came back. They told the grieving woman beside the now still body of her only daughter that her husband had been mauled to death by a wounded bear and was not returning to their longhouse again. So Mahonoy was faced with the loss of the two people she loved most in her life on the same day and would now be alone at her cooking fire in the longhouse.

There was nothing she could do; Mahonoy had to part with her daughter who now walked a different trail with her father. While she was talking, the Indian woman had been stirring the squash soup and dishing it out. She placed some for Amelia into a hollowed out gourd bowl. Then she continued telling her sad tale, sitting down on a mat by Amelia until she had told of the whole tragic ordeal. A single glistening tear rolled down Mahonoy's cheek and she sighed and wiped it away. Then she was silent except for the sound of the hot soup she sipped right from the bowl. She stared off into the distance toward the animal skin that covered the door, longing for one of her loved ones to push back the entrance and come in.

Amelia didn't know what had made Mahonoy so sad, but she felt a tenderness and empathy for the Lenape woman who spoke in such a gentle voice to her. The thick squash soup tasted warm and good. She felt awkward drinking right out of the bowl like that and even dribbled some down her chin, but it was filling and felt comforting and warm in her empty stomach. When they were done with their meal, Mahonoy gathered up the bowls and some cooking utensils and started out of the longhouse. Amelia sat still on the mat; she was so tired, she just wanted to rest. Mahonoy turned around and motioned for her to follow. Amelia didn't move, so Mahonoy came back over to her and, tugging onto her shoulder, pulled her to her feet saying "ikalichi," move. Then she said something else forcefully to Amelia that made her understand she was to follow, now! Amelia was just beginning to feel safe inside the longhouse, away from Shomachsom and the prying eyes of the others. She didn't want to go back out there, but she obeyed Mahonoy. The Indian woman gave her the gourd bowls to carry saying "këlënëmai," and led Amelia back toward the stream. Lenape children saw Amelia was back outside and started running around the woman and child as they walked toward the water. Amelia heard them call out Indian names to her and saw them laugh. Mahonoy stopped and spoke sharply to them and they settled down, just watching and walking alongside. But they still continued to whisper to each other and giggle after a few moments. Amelia was watched closely as she walked along. These Indian children hadn't seen many white people before, especially a young girl dressed so strangely. Amelia saw Mahonoy kneel down by the water and start rinsing out the utensils from cooking. She motioned for Amelia to kneel beside her and showed her how to rinse the gourd bowls in the stream. Mahonoy scooped up some water in a bowl, shook it some, and then let it spill back into the stream. All the while she talked to Amelia and repeated the Indian word for water "mpi." Amelia watched her face and listened as she repeated the word "mpi" to her several times. She realized Mahonoy was trying to teach her the word in her own language. Finally, haltingly, she said "mpi" back to her, which instantly brought a smile to Mahonoy's face. Then she nodded her approval to Amelia and to the children still watching them. After that they left the creek with the clean gourd bowls and went back to the longhouse of Mahonoy.

Once inside, Amelia sat right back down on the mat. She was so weary from the traveling and what she had been going through. She silently watched what was going on in her new surroundings. Other Indians came in through the outside door, said something to Mahonoy in a very respectful manner, and then disappeared to another part of the longhouse. Amelia was beginning to understand that the longhouse was a place several people lived, with rooms separated by partitions. It was late and Mahonoy raked coals together in the fire for the night and cleaned up her cooking area. Amelia watched her work and looked closer at the middle-aged woman's attire. She had a soft leather skirt on that came halfway to her ankles. It appeared not to be tight or hard to move in, although it was made of deer hide. The hem of it was cut all around into narrow fringe that hung around her ankles like tassels. On her body she wore a loose fitting tunic that came down over the top of the skirt. It was made of the same type of deer skin. The tunic had no sleeves to it and the neckline of the top was just an opening cut straight across for the head to go through. It was fringed along the bottom of it also. The waist was cinched in by a belt tied into a knot. She wore a small pouch decorated with beads on a long leather thong around her neck that hung down like a pendant. Her hair had been black but now was streaked with grey, straight and long. She had a fabric headband tied around her forehead with some geometric decorations and feathers tied on it that hung down by the side of her head. On her feet were moccasins that had tops coming halfway up to her knees. Amelia thought she recognized silver coins with holes drilled in them sewn onto the moccasins as decorations along with some colorful beads. Mahonoy's hands were the hands of a woman who had done hard work. Her fingers were broad and had knarled knuckles and short, clean nails. Occasionally, when she moved to lift something, Amelia heard a sigh escape her lips and realized Mahonoy lived with the physical pain of aging. Her face was deeply lined and had a look of sadness about it that contrasted with the laugh lines around her eyes.

Mahonoy finished tidying up, took a broom made of corn husks tied together and swept the dirt floor. She removed all the footprints from their walking and left a smoothed out area around the fire. Then she came over to Amelia and once again pulled her to her feet. She took her hand and led her to one of the benches along the wall of the longhouse, into the sleeping section. She spread out some rolled up furs and motioned for Amelia to lie down. By that time Amelia could hardly keep her eyes open and was glad to be sleeping inside that night, so she quickly obeyed and lay down to rest on the rough bed platform. It was very dark now in the longhouse. The cooking fire had burned down low. Amelia could see it was a moonlit night through the smoke hole opening in the roof. Other than that, no light came through the bark walls to the inside of the longhouse. Lying there in the quiet, she heard the subdued voices of other Indians talking elsewhere in the longhouse now, and then only silence. Later, close by, she thought she heard the muffled sound of a woman quietly weeping in the dark, and realized it was Mahonoy.

CHAPTER 9

A MELIA WOKE THE NEXT MORNING TO the sound of happy children playing outside. She opened her eyes and saw the bottom of the pallet above her and noticed that all the wood saplings had been lashed together with vines and had no nails to hold them tight. She turned her head toward the wall and saw the morning light peaking here and there between the shingled bark sides of the longhouse. Something smelled good and it urged her sore body to get up and investigate. The sapling pallet she had rested on wasn't cold and damp like the ground in the woods, but she had felt every bumpy stick of it last night before she mercifully fell asleep. It was going to take something to get used to, a bed as hard as that. Amelia's own bed back at the cabin had been rustic, but it did have a mattress stuffed with corn shucks, milkweed down, grass, dried moss, and anything else they could find to fill it with before it was stitched closed. Here, the Indians slept right on the small sapling sticks they lashed together with only a thin fur animal skin or a thin mat over the wood as a covering.

Amelia sat up. Her head almost touched the bottom of the pallet above her. She swung her feet out and stood up in the aisle. Mahonoy noticed her movements and called out to her with Indian words that meant something like she was a sleepy head. Mahonoy was stirring a simmering cooking pot on a stick tripod over the fire. Amelia yawned and stretched her arms. She was stiff and sore all over. She hesitantly walked out into the larger room. Mahonoy nodded at her and spoke in Indian words again, then took a ladle and dished out something that looked like porridge into a gourd bowl. Mahonoy held it out to Amelia saying "wisaminii," and nodded her head. Amelia took it, said thank you to Mahonoy, and sat down cross-legged on the mat by the fire. Mahonoy dished herself out some of the porridge and sat down across from her. Amelia was looking for a spoon to eat with but couldn't see any in the things around them. Mahonoy let her dish of porridge cool a little and then stuck in a couple of fingers and scooped some out and ate. She smacked her lips and motioned to Amelia to do the same thing. Amelia had woken up hungry and the food smelled good to her. Despite the warnings of her own mother to always hold her spoon like a young lady, she plunged her fingers in, scooped some out like Mahonoy and tasted the food. It was a yellow grain, starchy, bland, and somewhat gritty. She decided from its color that it must be ground corn meal, perhaps soaked in water and then cooked. She had eaten something like it before, only it had been not so coarse, sweetened, and sometimes her family even had some milk to put on it. Always though, she had used spoons and forks to eat. Amelia was not fond of the bland taste of the breakfast or the way she had to eat it but made the best of what she had. Hunger on the trek through the woods had taught her to take what she could get for food.

After they finished breakfast, Mahonoy again gathered together the cooking items. Then she went into the sleeping area and got a rolled up bundle that was tucked away against a wall. She took Amelia out the door of the longhouse and they went back to the side of the stream. This time they both went further up the waterway to a place sheltered from the sight of the village by bushes and trees. Mahonoy sat her bundle down, and she and Amelia washed the morning dishes. When they were done, Amelia turned to go back to the longhouse but Mahonoy stopped her. She started pulling at Amelia's clothes, trying to get her to take them off. Mahonoy's actions were frightening Amelia but her soothing tone and persistence soon made Amelia understand she should take her dirty clothes off and get into the cold creek water to bathe. Amelia followed directions and was just finishing undressing when another Indian woman and some younger children came walking into the same area and joined them. The children quickly stripped off their clothes, and uninhibited, plunged splashing and laughing into the water. Amelia waded out; each careful step took her deeper into the icy, swift, stream.

Once there, her body got used to the numbing cold and she seized the chance to wash her hair and clean herself for the first time in days. She had many old and new bruises on her body as well as scrapes and scratches from traveling through the woods. The water actually felt good on her injuries. She looked back at the bank and saw Mahonoy unrolling the bundle she had brought along. When Amelia was ready to come out of the water, Mahonoy had a warm, soft blanket waiting for her. She helped her dry, and while she was doing that, the other children left the water too and quickly dressed. Then they started going through Amelia's clothes lying on the ground and taking them. Amelia tried to stop them and shouted "No, they're mine. Leave them alone!" and moved toward the children to get her clothes. But Mahonoy stood firm in front of her, helping her to dry and blocking her way. Mahonoy tried to calm her with a gentle "shh . . . shh." Then she reached down to where she had spread open the bundle she had brought from the longhouse. She lifted up an amber colored tunic made from soft deerskin and gave it to Amelia to put on. There were also beaded moccasins to go with it. One of the Indian children had grabbed Amelia's shoes and put them on his hands. He banged the soles together, making noise, and glanced mischievously toward Amelia and then took off in the direction of the village with them. Another little girl ran off too, dragging Amelia's nightgown in the dirt behind her as she went. Still others were having a tug of war with her cloak. Amelia had no choice, her clothes were gone. She had to put on the Indian garments that Mahonoy had brought her to wear or be naked.

She quickly dressed and was surprised at how soft the garments were against her skin. They were smooth on the outside and on the inside, it had a soft nap like flannel cloth. Mahonoy pointed to a large rock and motioned for Amelia to sit down. Then she took out a comb made from bone and started combing Amelia's hair. She listened to Mahonoy talking gently to her in her Indian tongue as she tried to get the snarls and tangles out. It hurt because Amelia's hair was so knotted from the days of neglect. Sometimes it sounded as if Mahonoy was apologizing to Amelia for pulling on her hair so much. The Indian woman touching her hair did not repulse Amelia like the thought of touching Shomachsom's hand had. Mahonoy had a comforting, motherly touch and Amelia already felt safe with her, and cared for. She could see the tenderness in Mahonoy's eyes when she looked at her dark face. When they headed back for the village, it was not as easy for anyone to tell Amelia from the other Indian children except for her white skin. Mahonoy had parted and braided Amelia's hair, tying the ends with leather thongs. They passed some children tugging hard on Amelia's stolen nightgown. They ripped it in two, but Amelia ignored them now. She felt like a pampered princess with a freshly bathed body, groomed hair, and new clothes.

Mahonoy kept Amelia close by her side in the days and weeks that followed. Amelia learned the chores of the women and children of the village. They tended the corn and other vegetables, went out into the woods and fields to gather wild food, and prepared and cooked the meals. They worked the skins of the animals the men killed until they were soft leather. Then they used them for sewing into clothing and other uses. Hours and hours were spent making intricate, colorful, beaded designs as decorations on garments and sacred objects. Sometimes the women would travel to a spot on the River of Pines that had clay in the bank. They would dig the clay and knead it into a ball. Often they added finely ground, fresh water mollusk shells to make it stronger. They formed the clay into pots to use as storage vessels or for cooking meals. After burying the dried clay pots in layers of wood, they set the pile on fire and kept it going for hours until the pots became hard and durable. The Lenape women also cut long strips of bark from trees by scoring it with a knife and pulling it off from the trunk upwards. After that they cut the strips even narrower and wove them into storage containers and gathering baskets. There was plenty to keep an Indian woman busy every day. Just gathering and preparing food took up a good part of their time.

The men hunted and fished for other food. They were constantly making new points for the arrows they needed to hunt with and would take long journeys to get the stone blanks to chip them out of. They carefully chose strong, straight branches from hard wood to use for arrows. It took time to shave down the shanks to make the arrows into smooth, straight missiles and attach the feathers and tips so they would go straight to their targets. They had to make special points for different game. Small points were for birds or fish, and larger, stronger points were made for deer and other game. Bows had to be crafted from tough wood that could be bent and still hold the tension needed for hunting. Strings had to be prepared from the sinew of deer and elk. They also spent time chipping notches into flat, round stones to use as sinkers to tie their nets onto for fishing. Sometimes they had to make repairs to the longhouse and cut big chunks of bark to use as the shingles. There were a few highly prized hatchets in the community that were used for that purpose. Most of the rest of their primitive tools were hand-crafted and made of bone, wood, and stone.

Amelia remembered her father's precious assortment of hand tools he worked with and was amazed at what the Indians had to use for working. Men also had duties as the spiritual leaders of the community. Spiritual masks had to be made for the several ceremonies throughout the year. Some of the masks were made of finely woven strips of cornhusks, but others were carved from the trunk of a living tree to make them powerful with the tree spirit that lived there. Men also took care of Indian council matters. Amelia learned the women, however, were very important and powerful in the community, and could choose or remove the men from council if they wanted.

The children helped in all the chores of the community. After doing their own chores, they freely moved from one family to another to do whatever seemed interesting to them that day. The men and women elders of the group would tell the children stories as they worked, whether they were making baskets, chipping arrowheads, gathering food, or making repairs to the longhouse. That's how Lenape children learned of the Indian ways. Amelia was kept so busy during the day her thoughts were mostly on what she was doing and learning. But when the longhouse became quiet at night, she longed for her mother, father, and brothers back at her cabin home and often cried herself quietly to sleep wanting to see them so much.

Amelia was grateful she didn't see much of the Indian Shomach-som. When two white traders with packhorses came to the village one day, Mahonoy kept her inside the longhouse out of sight. She didn't want them to know they had a white captive. Some of the visitors spoke an unfamiliar sort of English. Amelia understood a little of the conversation about trading goods as she tried to listen through the wall of the longhouse. She was more afraid of the rough looking type of men that had long, dirty, shaggy beards and unkempt hair. They carried big rifles and wore wide leather belts with bullets and heavy knives hanging on them. Their clothes looked as if they lived in them, as they did, and were an assortment of animal furs, leather garments, and crudely woven rough cloth. They entered the village with a small string of packhorses laden down with heaps of fur, banging pots and pans, and other assorted goods tied onto the horse's backs. Amelia didn't even attempt to break free and alert them she was there. The rough looking, white strangers made her feel very uncomfortable. It was good Mahonoy had kept her inside that day when the curly blond-haired scalp and beaver skins were traded for the metal kettles, hatchets, and guns.

When Amelia was in the longhouse hiding with Mahonoy, the Indian woman brought out a palm sized small leather pouch decorated with glass bead flowers and fringe. It was attached to a leather thong, like a necklace, and she put it over Amelia's head. Mahonoy's eyes glistened with moist tears as Amelia thanked her for the gift. After Mahonoy left, she looked inside the little pouch to see what it held. She found a tiny canoe fashioned out of beaten copper, and a little miniature doll figure crafted from finely woven cornhusk strips. She turned them over and over in her fingers, marveling at the tiny, delicate workmanship. At that time she had no idea what they were for, or their meaning. Later, after she had made friends with the other Indian children she found out they were highly prized wish tokens. Lenape often carried miniatures of things they wanted to have someday. Mahonoy was wishing that someday Amelia would have her own canoe and children. Amelia was extremely touched by Mahonoy's gesture when she understood its meaning. Sometimes the other children would trade their wish tokens, but Amelia always held on to her gift from Mahonoy.

CHAPTER 10

AS THE DAYS AND WEEKS WENT by, Amelia became more and more like a Lenape Indian child and less of a colonial girl. Her mind protected her from the deep sadness of losing her family by making her into someone else. Occasionally she would still think of her home, but there was so much work to do before winter that she was often just too busy. Some of her chores included the tedious job of grinding corn. She had to rub the dried kernels off the cob and put some into a bowl-like depression on a large grinding stone. Then she had to use another stone to push the kernels back and forth until they were turned into a coarse cornmeal. It was slow work, and there was a lot of corn to do. She had learned several Indian words because of the patience of Mahonoy and the other children friends she had made. Now she could understand what others were saying as well as join in the conversations herself.

When they tried to give her an Indian name, however, she stubbornly refused to answer to it. She repeated that her name was Amelia so many times that eventually they gave up trying to change her name. The Indians had respect for people who did not waver under pressure. It was important to Amelia that she keep that part of her identity. They had trouble pronouncing her English name correctly though, and eventually, she accepted the new name they called her as close enough. It was Ah-me-ya.

Mahonoy was always so patient and understanding with her. She never punished Ahmeya for doing anything wrong, she just showed her again and again how it was supposed to be done. All the Indian children were given freedom to explore everything. If a child was interested in the fire they were allowed to get close to it and play with it if they wanted. If they received a minor burn, they learned it was dangerous to be by fire. Of course, they were protected from serious harm, though. Ahmeya saw how Indian families doted over their children. They lavished them with love, tenderness, and tolerance. When Ahmeya was troubled with nightmares, Mahonoy made her a dream catcher to hang by her head as she slept. It looked like a web of strings on a hoop with feathers hanging at the bottom. It trapped the bad dreams, but let the good ones trickle down the feathers onto the person who slept beneath it.

There was another Indian woman in their longhouse that had a small girl about the age of her baby brother, Christopher. Ahmeya was trusted enough now to watch the child while the women worked. She liked the responsibility and hugged, loved, and played with the little girl as if she were her own sister. Ahmeya made her a doll from a corncob that had a cornhusk skirt and Indian style tunic with long strands of corn silk for hair. She even made a tiny beaded necklace for the doll.

Soon the weather changed and the cold autumn winds came blowing into the village. It gusted between the longhouses and small clouds of dust billowed up and then quickly swirled away. Inside the longhouses were caches of food stored everywhere, back along the walls in baskets and pots and hanging from the ceiling in more containers. Yet the men still went out to hunt and the women kept busy stockpiling even more provisions. When it was too rainy to go outdoors and travel to hunt, fish, or gather, they all busied themselves inside. The men worked on their hunting equipment or maintained the structure of the longhouse. The women would roast some of the corn they had ground into a meal over the fire until it was a golden brown color. The men usually took some of it with them in a pouch when they traveled. They just soaked it in some water, and then ate it like a thick bread mush for nourishment. After the time of the winds that stripped all the leaves from the trees, the landscape became dismal shades of brown and grays. Flocks of geese were travelling south, and the skies wore broad horizontal strokes of slate colored clouds draped across them. Many of the songbirds disappeared. Sometimes when they woke in the mornings they could see their breath in the frosty air. Then the cold, blinding white snows arrived, forcing them to spend most of their time inside.

Some days they could go out all bundled up with fur shawls wrapped around them and get a little fresh air. Most days though, they were all stuck inside, trying to keep warm by the cooking fires and playing games or telling stories. The women cooked as usual, sewed new things, or made repairs to garments. It was a time to embellish clothes with beadwork designs. The Indian children would run quickly from longhouse to longhouse so they could visit their friends and spend time playing. Each time one went in or out the door, everyone yelled to close it quickly to keep the snow from blowing in. Ahmeya enjoyed playing a string game on her fingers with friends. She could make the shape of a tree and a fish and was learning to make more. She also played a game of sticks by dropping a bunch of small straight twigs so it made a heap and then carefully trying to take one out of the pile without disturbing the rest. It got harder and harder to do with each person's turn. She often ended up laughing along with her friends when she sent the whole pile tumbling. Many times, in the evenings, other Indian relatives from the longhouse would join Mahonoy at her fire and all would tell stories. They always asked Mahonoy to speak because she was such a wonderful storyteller. They begged her saying, "Achimwi, xaheli keku kuwatu." *Tell a story, you know many things.* She would give in and with animated face and hands, she walked around the listeners as her voice rose and fell with the telling of each story.

Ahmeya had learned enough of the language by then to understand the Lenape history stories. One cold evening Mahonoy told the story of the creation of the earth. Her steady voice recounted the sacred tale that her mother and her mother's mother had handed down, and at times her eyes glistened with a faraway look as she remembered other lodge fires long ago. It was a story of how they came to be.

"Before the sun shone, the sky was always dark. There was no man, no woman, no animals, nothing, but there was a great spirit Kishelamàkànk. He fell asleep and dreamed of trees and mountains and man. When he woke, he decided to create earth where our longhouses are. He created spirits of the north, east, west, and south to help, and together they made the earth and a special tree. From this tree the first man and woman came, and then tribes. After time terrible fighting came to the tribes and there was great wars between good and evil. Kishelamàkànk sent a sacred spirit Nanapush to earth. A great flood came to the forests and meadows and Nanapush climbed a mountain to escape. He grabbed the animals he saw, saving what he could. He started climbing a tall tree that grew at the top of the mountain as the water rose. All the land became water. Limbs were breaking off the tree Nanapush held onto. He asked the animals if any could float and turtle volunteered to save them. They piled sticks onto turtle's back and land began to grow. It needed to be bigger, so beaver and loon dove down to get mud, but muskrat got the most and the land grew larger and larger. Nanapush sent wolf out to see if he could find the edge of the new earth but he never returned. That is why wolf howls, calling for his ancestors he left behind. Kishelamàkànk thought the flood would end the battle between good and evil, but it still continues today."

Mahonoy stopped talking; the others just sadly nodded their heads in agreement. Then they said goodnight and left to their own area of the longhouse. Ahmeya had learned a lot about the people she now lived with. She saw the connection they had with the earth and its inhabitants. Everything had a spirit to them, even a rock, a tree, or the water. Yet, they had a fierce hatred for their enemies. She still did not know how they could kill and torture their enemies so cruelly and be so gentle and loving to their children and each other, but she too felt the same kinship with the woods and wild things. She had slowly become more and more like the Lenape around her

The winter was severe that year. Powerful icy winds thrust their cold massive bodies against the lashed together structures of the longhouses, making them sway and tremble. More than once she had awakened in the morning to find snow sifting through the cracks in the bark walls and falling onto her face. She'd bury herself down under the warm blankets of furs until Mahonoy would come to her and shake her to get up. She was teaching Ahmeya how to do some of the cooking chores now, and how to do sewing also. Winter was hard on all of them. Work still had to be done even in miserable weather. Wood was needed for fires and water had to be carried for cooking. Sometimes it meant breaking through the ice to get the water from the stream.

The men would get restless from being shut inside, and at the first sign of a break in the weather, they'd grab their hunting gear, bundle up with fur wraps, put snowshoes on, and head out. Marsh Creek was frozen over in most spots and they used it as a path to travel on. They set snares to catch the beaver and muskrats in the marshes that extended beyond the creek, then stretched and dried the pelts. The traders were always demanding more and more beaver skins and promised valuable goods in return. If the snow was too deep to travel into the woods, they'd sometimes hide behind bushes and trees along the banks of the creek and wait until they saw wolves chase a deer out onto the ice. The deer's smooth hooves were no good for running on ice, so when they slipped and fell, the wolves rushed in and attacked. Then the men, with loud shouts, clubs, and waving arms, would drive the wolves away from the freshly killed deer. They cut off big chunks of the venison for everyone in the camp and then left the remainder of the carcass to the wolves that watched, snarling at them from not far away. The fresh venison was a change from the rest of the dried winter provisions. The wild turkey they killed provided them with food and feathers for arrows and ceremonial attire.

If it were nice enough to stay out for a while, the men chopped a hole in the ice and fished, using string and hooks they had traded for. The trout they brought back were huge and gleamed with beautiful spotted patterns on their sides or colors like rainbows.

Isolated as they were, no strange visitors journeyed to their village during the deep snow to trade or sell goods. It was a time of tribal unity and sharing. Sometimes, however, there would be animated discussions among the men about the new settlers and the French and English who came to trade with them. They didn't really trust any of the non-Indians who spoke in lies. Often the women would step in and break up heated discussions between the men before it got out of control. Mostly though, they were a unified group and respected and cared for each other. They listened to each other's views, but held on strong to their own beliefs and opinions.

Ahmeya had learned during that winter how to use a lot of dried herbs and roots that had been gathered. Mahonoy used them in the foods that had been stored away and to make teas for colds and other ailments. Each time she thanked the earth for sharing its goodness with them. Ahmeya was eager to have Mahonoy show her the herbs growing wild when spring came, but that would be many weeks away yet. They still had to endure the worst months of winter. There were a few sunny and warm days in January, but then February came around with the worst of the biting cold weather, strong winds, and deep drifting snow. Sometimes the air was so cold it hurt the inside of Ahmeya's nose to breathe. March eventually arrived and the days alternated between cold winter and warm spring. During the sunlit days, snow melted, and at night the temperature dropped and froze to an icy landscape again.

To Ahmeya's surprise, one day, most of the tribe started gathering gear as if they were going on a trip. They packed provisions, dressed in their warmest clothes, and then set out on a trek into the mountains nearby. Only the very elderly or crippled stayed behind at the longhouses in the village. They travelled for a couple hours and then stopped in a large grove thick with mature maple trees. Mahonoy, Ahmeya, and the others set up camp in a flat area where there already were some small, dome shaped shelters made of saplings and covered with bark like their longhouses. The children scouted the area and picked up twigs and fallen branches for firewood. The women went to work unpacking pots and food and started cooking fires. The men then set out with their hatchets and after selecting the largest sugar maple trees, cut a big V about four feet up from the bottom. Ahmeya watched them at their work and saw them pound a hollow stick into a hole at the bottom of the V and hang a bark container on it. Later when the sun warmed the tree, the sap followed the cuts to the hollow stick and ran down inside it, filling the buckets to overflowing. They were collected each day and emptied into a large metal kettle over a fire. The Indians had paid dearly for that kettle. It had cost them many beaver pelts in trade, but was worth it. It was the women's job to keep wood on the fire, constantly stir the steaming kettle. and boil the sap down until it thickened and was syrupy. The air smelled wonderful with the scent of the maple sap boiling. Most of it was cooked right down to a sugar. Sometimes they would dribble the hot thick syrup off the end of a stirring paddle onto a clean white patch of snow. It would instantly harden into strings of maple candy and the children would pick it up and eat it as soon as they could touch it. The women didn't do that very much though because the sugar was so precious to them. The days started to get warmer and the maple sap didn't run as well and fill the buckets. After a couple weeks, the reddish leaf buds started to burst out and there was very little sap dripping down into the bucket. The time of the Maple Tree was over. They packed up what they had made and carried their precious maple sweetener back down to their longhouses by the River of Pines.

Spring had arrived with its awakening glory and the weather was getting better. Everything looked clean and fresh, bright and colorful. Canadian geese and other ducks had returned and were looking for nesting places along the streams. The wind started having some warmth to it. Everyone in the village was outside as much as they could be soaking up the sun after the long winter shut indoors. Mahonoy and Ahmeya hung the fur bedding outside in the fresh spring breezes over racks. Children raced around again and played their games and the morale of the tribe was high. It was the Time of New Life, when the leaves burst out and the forest was green with fresh growth again. Mahonoy took Ahmeya to the woods to gather wild herbs. She taught her about the medicine of the yellow flowered coltsfoot that bloomed first in the spring. She showed her the hooded Jack in the Pulpit that grew close to streams and how to use its peppery medicine. She dug up the small potato-like nuggets of delicate, pink Spring Beauty for roasting and eating later. Mahonoy showed Ahmeya the small leaves of the trailing Squawberry used to make a tea for women and had her taste the Sweet Black Birch bark to chew for the stomach. Mahonoy, like the other Indian women, knew all the plants and trees of the forest and thanked their spirits for allowing their use. She and Ahmeya filled a basket with an assortment of plants, roots, and pieces of bark. Mahonoy often spoke reverently to the trees she passed by calling out their names and thanking them for being there.

When it was time to leave, Ahmeya could not see the path and got confused. She was all turned around from where she thought she was and started heading off in the wrong direction. Mahonoy called her back laughing, saying she was like a rabbit that ran such a zig zag path he forgot how to make a straight trail home. She told Ahmeya to follow her and led the way out of the woods, teaching her all the time about how to find the right direction by the moss on the trees and other signs. Ahmeya was grateful for her guidance to the longhouse. Most of the things they gathered that day were bundled, tied, and hung from roof poles in the longhouse to dry in the warm air. Later that spring, the men broke ground with hoes made of parts of deer and elk antlers lashed to sticks with rawhide. It was the Time of the Planting. The women and children dug holes and planted the seeds of corn, squash, and beans they had saved from last year's crops. Often, they used a fish for fertilizer by tossing it in the hole with the seeds before they covered them with earth.

The white traders started coming to the camp again to trade for the bounty of winter furs the men and women had prepared. Mahonoy always kept Ahmeya out of the sight of their prying eyes. The traders were always on the lookout for captives they could trade for and resell at a good profit to the grateful families who were looking for their family members. It didn't bother Ahmeya that she was kept hidden each time the strangers came. By then, she felt she was a Lenape girl; she loved Mahonoy like a mother and had developed a strong loyalty and connection to the people of her longhouse.

During summer, the men went hunting and Mahonoy and Ahmeya, like the other women, cared for the crops, the cooking, gathering, and making garments. A group of them would often go together to gather berries in the woods and picnic. That was a pleasant chore and a fun outing Ahmeya always enjoyed. Ahmeya also swam in the stream and played games with the other children. She learned how to skillfully throw a corncob that had feathers stuck into it through a small hoop suspended from a limb. The other children would make it harder to hit the target by making the hoop swing from side to side. At first, she was terrible at the game and she withstood the laughter of the others as her timing was off and she missed the hoop again and again. Eventually though, she got the timing right and from then on, she could compete with any of them.

It was amazing to her that Mahonoy made everything she and Ahmeya needed from what was around them in the woods and meadows. She made the clothes they wore and their moccasins from the hides of deer and elk. Their jewelry was made from shells, bone, glass beads, and even coins from traders. The glass beads and coins came from trading what they hunted and trapped. Their utensils were carved from gourds they grew and dried, or from wood carved into stirring paddles. She gathered their medicine and grew corn, beans, and squash for their food. She and Ahmeya washed in the cold, clear stream water and softened their skin with animal fat. They did all this with a grateful thank you to the Earth Spirit for providing generously and sharing all it had with them.

CHAPTER 11

AND THAT'S HOW AHMEYA SPENT THE next few years of her life living with Mahonoy in the Indian village of the Lenape at the Great Meadows. With each changing season, they did the labor survival required for that time of the year, but it wasn't all work. They had many ceremonies to celebrate events such as the Time of the Maple Tree or Strawberry, the Blueberry harvest, or the Corn Grinding. There was a reason to celebrate and dance and sing songs for every season of the year, but the changing seasons brought many chores to do also. They were always busy making new clay pots to replace ones that had been broken or to make more for storage. The woman decorated them with scribed designs of straight parallel lines in the damp clay, patterns their ancestors had taught them. When the pots were dried thoroughly, they were carefully stacked together. They heaped firewood over and around the pile of pots and lit the fire. They had to keep piling on firewood for several hours to keep the flames burning hot before finally letting it die down to just embers. Later they would pull the blackened, charred pots out of the cooled ashes and wipe them clean. Pottery making was a skill that had been taught from mother to daughter for many generations. But, when the traders brought them tin and brass pots for cooking, they made progressively fewer clay ones. The men had always made bows and arrows for hunting, but when they started trading beaver skins for the powerful, loud guns to kill game, they set aside their bows and used them less often. The worst vice that the traders introduced to the village though was rum, and as a result, fights broke out among the Indian men. The women had to break the fights up to keep peace in the tribe. Before the traders, they had been able to provide for all their needs. Now they wanted the metal pots, guns, and the rum that made them crazy and dangerous to each other.

One day after the men had been gone hunting for a few days, they returned very agitated and loud. A whole new wave of settlers was in their hunting grounds, they announced angrily to all those gathered around them. The settlers had moved into an area to the east now, just a few days away from their longhouses. Also, an Indian trader they met on the trail told them the white chief Washington was paying money for the scalps of Indian men and women. Mahonoy and the other woman decided it was time to call a council meeting and ask for advice from their elders to the north. A wampum belt was quickly made and sent with a runner to the land of the Seneca beyond the mountains to the north. What should they do, they all wondered, as they waited for a message from their elders? Should they stay and fight the intruding colonists? Should they leave their longhouses and move further west? Should they join their brothers, the Seneca, up north in the big lake country? What if more armed settlers moved even closer to them? Their future seemed uncertain and dangerous.

The people of the Lenape village had been uprooted and pushed out too many times already and were angry that the settlers thought they could just take what had been their ancestors' land and game from them. They couldn't understand why they didn't go back where they came from and leave them alone. The Lenape were happy where they were now; they had few enemies nearby. They had everything they needed to live well. The remoteness of their location on the River of Pines had so far protected them from intrusion. But, they also feared they would be caught in the middle of a war between the tribes of the French, English, and the colonists. The unscrupulous traders were pushing them to get more and more pelts, and lately, even scalps for buying goods. The traders were under pressure to provide beaver pelts to make fashionable top hats and coats for the English. The traders also made money by turning in Indian scalps. They urged the Lenape to take scalps from any French they came across and the Indian scouts who travelled with them, even the scalps they had taken fighting other tribes.

Despite their best efforts to keep their village as it was, the white man kept inching closer, causing strain and tension in the once-peaceful life of the tribe.

Ahmeya had been so happy earlier in the day. She sat on a warm, smooth boulder in the sun by the stream and watched river otters playing in the water. They chased each other like children being "it" and swam as free and unencumbered as the swallows soared in flight. They'd swim side by side and then separate and head off in opposite directions. Next, they quickly dove down into the depths of the water and arched back to wrestle with each other all over again. Their wet brown fur was shiny and sleek and they had big, dark marble eyes with a muzzle full of long, sensitive whiskers. They were so comical to watch as they played. Ahmeya laughed at them and they stopped playing, looking at her as if they were thinking, "What's so funny?" Then they forgot about her and went right back to playing with each other again.

The Indian runner that had been sent off to the north returned in a couple days with a wampum belt from the people of the land of the Seneca. They agreed that a council should be held. The Seneca would journey down in six moons to meet with them at the Great Meadow. Preparations started to be made in the village and every-one talked excitedly about the upcoming event. They had guests coming, very important guests. Food had to be planned and sacred ceremonial clothes and gear had to be taken out and readied. The men went fishing and the women busily cleaned the longhouses and cooked what could be prepared ahead of the visit. Ahmeya, Mahonoy, and everyone anxiously and curiously awaited the Sen-eca visitors. The children were kept busy collecting firewood and piling it up. There would be many council fires late into the night for talking.

When the Seneca arrived by canoe, everyone in the village hur-ried down to the water's edge to greet them. Dogs were barking and men, women, and children came out of their longhouses with arms waving and shouts of welcome. The Indian delegation from the Seneca consisted of six men who traveled in three large birch bark canoes. These Seneca Indians looked much the same as the Lenape, Ahmeya thought. One man stood out among the others in stature though, and she recognized him as Constayunka, the Indian who had kidnapped her and her family several years before. He was a distant relative of Shomachsom and that is why they had been together scouting and raiding in the area of her cabin years before.

The guests were welcomed into the longhouses and soon given something to eat. There was to be no talk of council matters until that evening to give them a chance to rest and clear their thoughts. The meal for supper that night was wonderful. Meaty rabbits and plump pheasants were roasted on a spit over the fire until they were tender and smoky flavored, with juices dripping from them. Squash had been baked in the coals and then cut open and the orange flesh was sprinkled with some of the precious maple sugar made in the spring. They also had a type of bread made of ground cornmeal and some stewed dried apples. It was a feast and everyone stuffed themselves. They sat eating around the outside fires and enjoyed each other's company, talking of less serious things. By the time the meal was finished, it was dark. The cooking things were picked up and the women went to the stream to wash them and freshen up. They whispered nervously to each other, wondering what was to happen that evening. When they returned, the men of the village had all changed into their ceremonial regalia. Ahmeya was in awe of some of the clothing they were wearing. They were adorned with feathers and intricate beads and flashed with pounded copper and silver coins. The women quickly changed into their best outfits also. Important decisions were to be made; they needed to dress with respect to their ancestors and bring harmony and honor to the presence of their guests.

Constayunka had not given any sign he recognized Ahmeya. She looked so like an Indian now. Her skin had tanned deeply due to all the outdoor activities she did. She wanted to go up to him and ask him questions. She wondered if her mother lived with him in the Seneca land, but she was prevented from talking to him directly due to his status as a visiting dignitary. Constayunka was now also dressed in full Indian regalia suitable for discussing critical matters. Around his forehead was a beaded and decorated suede headband. On top of his head were large eagle feathers that pointed in opposite directions and some smaller feathers among them fanned out so that the whole top of his head was crowned with feathers. His straight black hair was tied into two long locks that fell forward over his shoulders and onto his chest. By each ear, there was a large hammered silver disk attached to his hair locks. Then below that, his hair was wrapped with a crisscrossing leather thong, and just before the end of each hair lock, there was another smaller silver hammered disk. He wore necklaces of drilled bear claws and another of a large silver gorget that lay across his chest like a shiny half-moon. He also had strings of small, multi-colored beads that were a mixture of glass and shell. His tunic was decorated with red and black geometric patterns, many porcupine quills, and more beaded designs. Over his leggings of golden suede deerskin, he wore a sort of short apron with a design that looked like a sun with rays coming off it. His high-topped moccasins came up to his knees and were beaded all around the top with diamond patterns. Cut leather fringe ran down the outside of his moccasins to his ankles. Around each wrist he wore a wide bracelet band that was completely covered with beaded designs. Over one shoulder he carried a woolen blanket that hung loosely down his back and was draped over his other arm which held up the end of the blanket. He was a striking and impressive sight, and obviously he was a wise and important Indian dignitary.

The men and women of Ahmeya's village had all put on their best attire for the evening. A large, low drum had been brought out that was big enough for five men to sit around. The ceremony began with the blessing of the ceremonial drum. Sacred tobacco was sprinkled onto the drum by the Shaman. He also walked around with a cluster of smoking sage leaves in his hand to purify the air and the council members with smoke from head to toe. It was a night warm enough to have the meeting outside so everyone could see, and be a part of, what was happening at the gathering. The drummers began beating their deep, regular rhythm on the tightly stretched skin of the drum. One of the elders was responsible for leading the other drummers in song as they beat on the drum with intent seriousness. He raised his strong, baritone voice in solo Lenape song and then the others joined in and answered him. The first song was a call to the spirits of their ancestors to join them at the fire and share in their decision making. When the drumming began again, the male dancers started slowly moving in a circle around the fire in rhythm to the beat and chorus from the chanters seated around the drum. All the dancers had a fan of three or four eagle feathers they raised up to the sky as they danced in homage to the spirits. The dancing was not fast or erratic, or even particularly joyful. Like the music, the dancing was measured and rather somber in keeping with the seriousness of the evening's work.

The women did not dance with the men, nor were they allowed at the drum. The women did have a dance of their own and entered when the men left the circle. Ahmeya thought the women also looked wonderful clothed in their beautiful ceremonial dresses. Their long, soft deerskin dresses came all the way to their ankles and were generously decorated with geometric bead and porcupine quill patterns. The tops of their dance moccasins were intricately beaded as well. They wore cinch belts and necklaces adorned with more drilled shells and beads. All the women had worn their dark hair in braids and twisted into it were colorful ribbons. Round leather disks at the ends of their braids were covered with more geometric beaded designs. Most also carried a woven shawl with one end draped over their shoulder and the other end lay over their arm. A flat, fringed pouch with a long shoulder strap hung at their sides. Mahonoy and the other Indian women's dance and song were slow and seemed somber like the men's had been. They sang songs thanking the spirits for good harvests and of the loved ones whom they had lost. They danced until late into the night and then seeing their guests were very weary, they suddenly stopped. Everyone said goodnight and went to the longhouses to rest. The visitors were invited into different longhouses for the night and followed their hosts inside.

The next evening Ahmeya watched as the same scene was repeated and the men and women put on their best garments again. This time the dances were of shorter duration and then the visiting dignitaries and the council members gathered around the fire. They started calmly talking about the settlers moving into their territory, shooting and trapping so much game, and pushing them out. Ahmeya listened to their talk from a short distance along with the other Indian women. She realized that her family must have been some of the settlers they were talking about. The voices of the men started getting louder and more agitated as they talked of these matters. Some of the Lenape felt vengeful and wanted to go drive all the settlers away or kill them like the enemies they were and burn their dwellings. Others wondered if they couldn't possibly live side by side and be happy. The white people had many things to trade with them, they said, many things that made their life easier. Some spoke up and said they felt it was hopeless to stay because there were just too many settlers. They were killing all the game and they should go to the lands over the mountains to the west by the River O-Y-O. Constayunka, the Seneca, had brought other important members of the Iroquois confederation with him to speak with those gathered about these troubling matters. In the middle of the council circle, in the light of the fire, stood two upright poles with a longer pole resting horizontally between them. Over that long pole were several belts of wampum. Ahmeya saw each speaker come forward one at a time, take a belt, and tell the message that was recorded on it in beaded designs. One of the Seneca speakers was especially animated and Ahmeya listened carefully to his words. He said that the Lenape elders had signed over the land they had been living on years earlier in a treaty and been paid goods for it. They had made a deal with the white chiefs. The land was no longer the hunting grounds of the Lenape and they had to leave or the white man would kill them, attack other tribes, and cause problems with the Iroquois. Their warriors would be killed and their women and children would starve or be taken and used as slaves for the English. The Lenape were infuriated by his remarks. Several jumped up and were shouting at the speaker. How could their elders give away their valuable hunting land, the land of their longhouses? Where were they to go, and why should they do what the Seneca wanted? At that, the Seneca dignitaries asserted their power and status and told them they were not brothers or sisters of the Seneca, but cousins instead. They had to obey the will of the powerful Iroquois Nation or face harsh discipline from them. Ahmeya heard him say the Lenape must move off the lands they no longer had a right to be on, as soon as possible, or risk the wrath of the colonists and the Iroquois Nation. Ahmeya waited and watched anxiously as the Lenape elders talked with each other, trying to decide what to do. Their disappointment and confusion were evident and worry showed in the expressions on their faces.

The discussions between the Seneca visitors and the Lenape council members went on for days. In the end, the Lenape were split into two groups. Some decided to go north to live in the Seneca lands. Others would go west to find new hunting grounds over the mountains to live, but all had accepted that they could no longer live in their longhouses by the River of Pines. That Indian community and the longhouse where Ahmeya had grown to feel safe and happy would be no more.

CHAPTER 12

MAHONOY CHOSE TO MOVE HER FAMILY to the land of the Seneca, The Keepers of the Western Gate. They took what they could carry in baskets or bundles and sadly said goodbye to their familiar longhouses. Ahmeya looked back wistfully at the gardens, the apple orchards, and the River of Pines where she had gone swimming with her friends, played, and grown. She looked at the tall mountains covered with pines and maples and hickory. She thought of all the woodland trails she had travelled with Mahonoy and her friends gathering herbs and berries. They had lived there in peace and harmony for many years, but now it no longer was to be their place of sanctuary.

Ahmeya and Mahonoy would have to travel a long way to get to their new place to live. Some of it would be by the waterways. A lot of traveling would involve walking over land. It would be dangerous with all the new settlers, French, and other strangers now in the territory that they had to avoid contact with. Ahmeya had spent nine years growing up as Mahonoy's adopted daughter and had become a beautiful and respected young Indian woman. She was just as sad as the rest of the people of the longhouses that they were parting company and moving where many of them would never see each other again, but they couldn't dwell too long on the separation and departure. They needed to think about their future, their new longhouse and getting settled back into a safe, normal life as soon as possible.

Ahmeya wondered with each step northward if it would be much different where they were going. What would the Seneca be like? Would they really welcome the Lenape to live by them? Lately, Ahmeya had also been wondering about her own future. She was a woman now. None of the braves at the River of Pines had interested her romantically; she thought of them all as her brothers. Was she destined to be an old maid squaw with only a fire to keep her warm and relatives to tend to? It was scary leaving everything that was familiar to her. She was leaving the safety of the familiar longhouse with all her friends and relatives living close by. She thought of the cold winter evenings when they had all gathered around the fire. Together they had listened to the elders tell stories of their past and the spirits of the earth, sky, and animals. With each hunting story, creation story, or funny incident they told and retold by the firelight, they had all listened, shared, and bonded.

Ahmeya thought of all these things as she traveled north with the small band of her Lenape family members. They traveled along Marsh Creek until they came to the junction of the Teaoga River. From there they turned north and followed the river, which crossed the end of a large lake. Then they went on up to where it joined another river and a branch headed northwest to the shore of Seneca Lake. It took them a week to get there, walking constantly from early morning until dusk every day. They were headed to where the Seneca Indians had an Indian castle of many cabins, gardens, and orchards along the shoreline of the lake. It was a beautiful country lying in the belly of a verdant green valley surrounded by rolling, heavily timbered hills and waterfalls that cascaded down glens and gullies. The Seneca were in many ways like the Lenape. However, the Lenape were a people proud of their own beliefs and of their independence. When they arrived, they decided they would build their own longhouses close to their northern allies for protection, but far enough away to have their own separate Lenape community.

They chose an area that was on a low, flat rise next to a feeder stream that ran into Seneca Lake. It was a good choice. The land didn't need much clearing and was fertile because it was low in the valley but high enough not to get flooded. Just beyond their clearing, the woods rose up thick and green, and they knew it must be full of game. The spot Mahonoy had chosen was also somewhat sheltered from the winds that blew across the lake. That was something they were grateful for the first winter in their new camp. The Seneca came to help them cut poles for the longhouse and strip bark. Ahmeya and Mahonoy gathered bittersweet vines and fine roots along with the other vines the women and men used for lashing poles together. With so many hands helping out, it wasn't long before Mahonoy and Ahmeya had a new roof over their heads. The Lenape were welcomed whole heartedly by their Seneca Indian friends, though the Lenape were considered a lower status than they in the Iroquois Nation. The Seneca brought them food and offered to share their apple orchards with them. Some of their braves offered to show the Lenape men how to go lake fishing because the Lenape were mostly used to fishing creeks and rivers.

It didn't take long for Ahmeya, Mahonoy, and the rest to settle in. Some of them, like Mahonoy and Shomachsom, were forced to move before. They had been pushed north or west more than once since the white man came to live on the frontier. The Indians knew little of colonial boundaries or owning land. To them, the land could not be owned; it was a spirit that allowed you to share in its gifts. It fed you and cared for you like a mother cares for its child. The whole concept of the white man owning everything and keeping it all for himself was strange to them. Ahmeya remembered some of the stories told at the campfires about the dreams the Indians had. Mahonoy had taught her it was their belief that if they dreamed something, it was a prophecy that was meant to be. So, when one of the braves dreamed he owned his friend's new hunting bow and told him that, he was given the bow. They were a generous and unselfish people, but the white man had changed much of that. It was the Lenape way to share everything with each other. The white man wanted it all for himself.

The path between the Seneca village and their new settlement was not long, and Seneca and Lenape freely traveled back and forth between the villages. They borrowed from each other and shared provisions. They got to know each other better with every day that passed. Everyone was making new friends, but Ahmeya was rather shy and kept somewhat to herself. Mahonoy had started exploring the woods for familiar plants and found many of the herbs, nuts, and berries they were used to growing in plentiful supply. The Seneca Indians had wonderful apple, peach, and cherry orchards that were generations old and well maintained that they gladly shared with the Lenape, giving them shoots to start their own orchards. They also knew how to launch their canoes into the often-choppy water of the big lake and paddle to spots where they could easily catch plenty of fish with hooks or by netting them. Sometimes they constructed traps to catch the fish migrating up the mouths of streams to spawn. The woods were full of elk, deer, rabbit, turkey, pheasants, and black bear. Life was very good there and Mahonoy and Ahmeya felt safe in the land of the Iroquois. It was a proud and powerful confederacy of different tribes of Indians joined together for strength, unity, and protection.

Ahmeya had a favorite spot beside one of the small streams in the woods. There the clear water cascaded down a rock and fern gully, running in cool rivulets that meandered off and joined the big lake. It was restful to sit beside the small stream and listen to the water running over the gray slate stones that wound down the gully in a series of rocky steps and small pools. Sometimes she tossed small leaves into the stream just to see them drift away and be swirled on a watery journey down the gulley. Ahmeya was sitting there one day in the early afternoon. She could feel the coolness of the large rock she was sitting on. She had her arms wrapped around her legs and her chin rested on her knees. She was lost in her thoughts watching small silver fish dart about between the rocks in the water at her feet. Then a movement below caught her attention. She saw a Seneca brave emerge from the woods and walk to a pool below to get a drink.

He didn't notice her because she was sitting so quietly in a sheltered spot out of his sight. Ahmeya watched him as he moved. All he wore on his lean and muscular body was a breechcloth and leather leggings protecting his shins and moccasins. He was bare from the waist up except for decorated leather armbands. A leather strap ran across his chest that held the quiver of arrows on his back. His black hair was pulled back away from his angular face. Some of it was tied up in a knot with eagle feathers on his head. He raised his arms over his head to remove his quiver of arrows and Ahmeya could see the muscles flex on his arms. His dark skinned body glistened with the bear fat he had rubbed on his skin. The lines of his face were noble Indian features with high cheekbones, a straight nose, and strong jaw line. He was altogether a handsome man to look at. Ahmeya could not take her eyes off him yet was frightened at the same time. Shifting her position, she moved her foot to see better and accidentally pushed a stone into the water that tumbled a short way down the stream stopping with a splash that got his attention.

Startled, the brave suddenly lifted his face from his cupped hands holding the water and looked upward in her direction. When Ahmeya's eyes met his, everything else in the forest became out of focus and all she saw was him. She was not looking just at a face, however. Instead she felt as if she was looking deep into his soul. Ahmeya felt an instant magnetism to him. Neither spoke and the forest was quiet. Time seemed to be suspended. All they heard was the sound of running water in the small stream. Somewhere a squirrel chattered loudly, breaking the trance, and Ahmeya, suddenly nervous, rose to go. The Seneca brave tried to halt her by calling out, "Stop . . . Wait." Ahmeya wanted to run away, escape, but something stronger made her stop and listen. She paused, waiting for him to speak again as she looked at him. "Who are you?" he asked. "What do they call you?"

"Ahmeya," she answered timidly. "My name is Ahmeya."

"Hmm," he replied, nodding his head. He too felt tongue-tied and at a loss for words all of a sudden. Silence again, just the sound of the running water passing by on a journey. Ahmeya, still nervous, moved to leave and the brave spoke again. "May I visit your longhouse?" he asked, calling up to her.

"Yes," was all she replied quietly after a pause. Then quickly she turned and disappeared into the thickness of the trees. He stood there looking at the spot where she had been. His puzzled reflection looked back from the pool of water. Ahmeya left the woods in a hurry on the path back to her longhouse. She realized she had never told the brave exactly where to come to visit or when. *How stupid I am!* She felt foolish for acting so flustered at his questions. *He must think I'm a silly little girl,* she thought. Ahmeya had never had these feelings before. She had connected with the spirit inside the brave just by looking into his eyes. She knew nothing about him, not how old he was, what he was like, or where he had come from. He must be Seneca, she knew that from his appearance and she was interested, very interested, in seeing him again. But also frightened.

By the time Ahmeya arrived at the longhouse, she had calmed down some. She entered with a smile on her face and a twinkling in her eyes that made Mahonoy curious right away. She good naturedly pestered Ahmeya to tell her what was pleasing her so, and before long everyone in the longhouse was teasing Ahmeya about the "mystery brave of the woods." Could she have been wish dreaming, they wondered playfully? No, he was real, living flesh; Ahmeya was sure of that. She blushed at the thought of watching him secretly. It was hard for her to sleep later that night; her mind was swimming with thoughts, new feelings, and questions.

CHAPTER 13

AHMEYA TOOK EXTRA TIME EACH MORNING to look nice, hoping the Seneca brave would visit her long- house. When he didn't show up at all the first week, she became discouraged. By the end of the second week, she had lost all hope of ever seeing him again. She was disappointed, but decided not to fantasize about the brave anymore and just keep herself busy with work. In the meantime, the men of her longhouse had gone to the lake fishing and brought home a catch of large fish. Mahonoy and Ahmeya were busy cutting off fish heads and gutting the carcasses in preparation for drying the strips of fish on racks in the sun. Ahmeya had fish blood and scales stuck to her hands and arms and was smelly from the work. She hung a raw filleted side of fish on the drying platform, reached for another, and when she looked up, the brave was standing there. He'd been watching her at work. Startled, she jumped and her thoughts started racing. She had that confusing feeling of wanting to run again and yet stay close to him at the same time. "Hè Ahmeya," he said with a funny grin on his face.

Ahmeya wiped her hand across her forehead, smearing fish scales and blood there as she did and just said "Humph." She tried to smooth her hair and make herself more presentable but all she managed to do was get fish scales stuck in her hair instead. Then she tried to clean her hands on her apron. "You came," she said, annoyed while sticking her nose in the air.

His soft but strong voice spoke to her. "I dreamed I caught a running deer deep in the woods and jumped onto his back. The deer raced through the forest. I had to hold on tight to its antlers to keep from falling off. I could not tell it where to go, and I could not make it stop when I tried. It raced out of the woods and came into a clearing where there was a longhouse. In my dream you were standing in the doorway smiling at me." Then he paused and said, still looking deep into her eyes, "How could I not come?"

Ahmeya understood dreams, they were meant to be, but she was still a woman and a stubborn and independent one at that. He had made her wait and worry for two weeks before he showed up, and she didn't even know the name of this brave standing before her. "Who are you?" she asked with a haughty tone in her voice.

"I am Tamataunee, a Seneca of the Turtle Clan."

Mahonoy heard the strange voice and suddenly appeared from behind the fish racks and said, "Oh, a visitor. You must be Ahmeya's mystery brave who drinks at the stream."

Ahmeya blushed; she didn't want the brave to know she had talked about him. She gave Mahonoy an annoyed look that said, please don't say anything else. But, Mahonoy just kept right on talking and smiling at the Seneca brave. She was feeding him questions trying to dig out more information about his background and relatives. Ahmeya, frustrated at them both, left and took the chance to wash up, all the time stealing glances back at the Seneca brave Tamataunee. *He's so handsome*, she said to herself as she washed. Tamataunee was glancing at her too, looking past Mahonoy's figure darting here and there, talking nonstop to him. Mahonoy knew, as a woman of the tribe and as his elder, that he would be respectful and listen and answer her questions all night if she chose to talk to him. "Come inside to our fire and share some drink with us," she said to him. She led the way into the longhouse and Tamataunee followed. Mahonoy called over her shoulder "You come too Ahmeya." By the time Ahmeya stepped inside, she had cleaned off most of the fish scales, straightened her hair, and looked presentable. Tamataunee was sitting on a mat and Mahonoy was pouring him something to drink.

"This is a happy longhouse," Mahonoy said. "The Great Spirit has been good to us. We are healthy and have plenty of food. Ahmeya is a wonderful daughter who works hard and obeys the Indian ways." Ahmeya blushed and gave Mahonoy another annoyed look. She was uncomfortable being talked about like that. Mahonoy urged, "Sit down Ahmeya, don't just stand there. We have a guest." Ahmeya sat down a short distance from Tamataunee. She wasn't close to him but she could feel the heat of his body and that scared, confusing feeling came back to her again. Everyone fell silent. Mahonoy and the brave both turned their heads and looked at her. Ahmeya knew by the tilting of Mahonoy's head and the prompting stare in her eyes that she wanted Ahmeya to speak.

Her mind was blank, confused, and she felt suddenly, utterly stupid. All she could think to ask him was, "How is the hunting, Tamataunee?" and she looked into the inviting soul of his dark eyes.

"The game is getting scarcer," he answered. "Too many hunters in the forest now; game is harder to get close to. I have to travel more than a day's journey away now to get elk and bear, but in my father's longhouse we have plenty." Then there was a long pause as no one spoke.

Then Mahonoy asked, "Tell me Tamataunee. On your hunts, did you ever see any little people in the forest?" Mahonoy and Tamataunee laughed at that question. Ahmeya didn't understand; she had never heard of any little people.

"Oh, you don't know about the small braves that live in the forest?" Tamataunee asked Ahmeya.

"No" she answered, "I've never heard of any small braves." She shook her head no again and looked at them both as if they were playing a trick on her.

Then Mahonoy urged Tamataunee on with, "Tell her, tell her the story of the braves of the forest."

Tamataunee started talking. He told a tale of a young Indian brave who was hunting in the woods one day. When he was walking through the woods he heard voices coming up from a dark ravine. Looking down, he spied two tiny men shorter than his knees. He had shot a squirrel earlier and offered it to the small men. They were so grateful, they invited him to dinner. They took him to their village and fed him corn soup from a gourd bowl that never emptied. They also gave him a round white stone to keep as a good luck charm for hunting. They called all the other Little People together to have a great feast. There were little squaws and children living there too. The little braves burned tobacco in a pipe and shared it with each other, and then they performed the sacred Dark Dance. The young Indian hunter watched in awe and studied their chants and gestures. Later he taught the dance to his own people. When it was time for the brave to leave, the Little People promised to come and visit the Indians with their invisible presence when the Indians played their drums and performed the Dark Dance. And that's how the Indians became friends with the Little People of the forest. They help control the forces of the wild things. Some of them are so strong they can upturn trees and hurl rocks. Some have the job of waking the sleeping plants each spring, and others have to watch the gates of the underworld to protect Indians from chaos and disease.

All the time Tamataunee had been telling the story, he and Mahonoy had been sipping at their drinks. Ahmeya had been so fascinated by the sound of his voice and watching his face, she was still holding a full cup in her hands. She had listened to him almost trancelike and now laughed at the funny, mystical story of the little braves along with them. Then sensing it was time for him to leave, Tamataunee turned respectfully to Mahonoy and rose to go, saying, "I must leave now."

"Visit our longhouse again Tamataunee. Visit again," Mahonoy said, touching his arm affectionately.

He walked to the door of the longhouse. Mahonoy was gathering the embers of the fire together and waved her hand for Ahmeya to go out with him. Ahmeya and Tamataunee stepped back into the sunlight. He reached out and took her hand, pressed a gift into it, and looked tenderly into her eyes. Then he quickly walked away, turned, looked back at her, and said, "I will dream again, Ahmeya." She opened her hand and looked down to see a beautiful white hair comb carved from an antler. On the handle was a silhouette of a deer drinking from a pool of water.

CHAPTER 14

THE NEXT TIME AHMEYA SAW TAMATAUNEE was by the creek where she and the others collected clay for pottery. She was with her best friend, Okawa. Ahmeya and Okawa did most of their chores together. Okawa was younger and usually talked too much, but Ahmeya enjoyed her cheerful nature. Today they were both over their ankles in the creek water scooping slippery grey chunks of clay off the bottom and tossing it onto the bank. The back hem of their suede skirts had been pulled forward between their knees and tucked into their waistbands at front. It gave them a sort of pantaloon type work outfit. Their hands and arms were coated with clay now and it looked like they had on grey gloves that went all the way to their elbows.

They worked with their feet placed wide apart for a firm stance on the slippery creek bottom. They had to feel around on the bottom for clay they could scrape loose because after a while the water became a swirling cloud of grey silt. Ahmeya hadn't told her friend yet that Tamataunee had visited her. Okawa was a fun person to be with but could tease Ahmeya relentlessly about any silly little thing. She knew Okawa would torment her with a thousand questions about Tamataunee and she wasn't ready to go through that ordeal yet, so she had kept him a secret.

The girls chatted about the pottery they were going to make, how much clay they needed to gather, and how they both liked forming the containers. It was almost mechanical the way they bent over, scooped the clay, then gathered it from the gourd scraper and tossed the chunks onto shore. Bend, scoop, twist, toss . . . bend, scoop, twist, toss . . . and then he was there standing silently like a statue on the shore.

Okawa was surprised to see him but, being naïve and mischievous, she had little fear of strangers, besides he was handsome. Ahmeya was slightly annoyed. It was the second time her brave had caught her doing a messy job.

"Hè Ahmeya," Tamataunee said looking at her.

"Hè Tamataunee," she greeted him back in the Lenape manner. Then Okawa realized that they knew each other and even more than that, she instantly sensed there was a strong attraction between the two.

"Hè . . . Hè . . ." Okawa said, mocking their greeting. She rolled up a ball of clay in her hands, leaned over, and bumped Ahmeya hip to hip almost knocking her down. "And what have you not told your best friend, Ahmeya?" she asked, all ready to start the teasing.

"Um . . . this is the Seneca Tamataunee I met in the woods a few weeks ago," she replied. You could see Okawa thinking about that statement and then a look of annoyance on her face. Okawa was getting angry that her friend had kept such juicy news from her. News she should have told her right away!

"Oh, so you met him a few weeks ago?" Okawa said in a mocking voice and flung the ball of clay onto the bank right at his feet. Tamataunee jumped back so it would miss his moccasins. "Eeya!" he shouted and looked at Okawa, perturbed. Ahmeya kept working but was uneasy about what might be coming next from her friend. Okawa slowly scooped up some more clay and made another ball. "And what is your brave doing here now, Ahmeya? Has he gotten lost, or perhaps he is thirsty?" And with that statement, she tossed another slimy ball of clay so close to his feet, grey silty water splashed onto his leggings. He wasn't happy about that. He liked to surprise Ahmeya by these "chance" meetings, but he had spent great care on making his appearance presentable to her.

He picked up a nearby rock and threw it into the water by Okawa, so she was the one who got splashed this time. And that was how it began. Ahmeya could only watch in horror as a contest of escalating challenges took place before her. Of course Okawa had to fling a bigger ball of clay at Tamataunee, but she didn't even try to miss his feet this time. And he had to retaliate with an even bigger

rock until it was an all-out war of splashing water and clay sling-
ing. Tamataunee and Okawa were so caught up in their contest
that they had forgotten about Ahmeya until they heard her shout,
"Enough!" The clay against rock splashing battle stopped suddenly
and they turned to see her sitting in the creek, wet from head to toe
with clay splattered on her hair, clothes, and face from their battle.
Sputtering, she attempted to stand and walk toward the shore as
they watched her like two guilty children. She almost made it, but
lost her footing on the bank and slid, arms flailing, face down back
into the muddy water.

Tamataunee rushed to help her and pulled her into a sitting position. She shook her head like a wet dog, took some deep breaths,
and then put both her hands against his chest and angrily shoved
him off balance into the stream too. Turning her back on them
both, she sputtered and said she "never, ever, wanted to see either
of them again!" Okawa and Tamataunee glared at each other as she
walked away.

It was awhile before Tamataunee dared to show up for another visit. By that time, Ahmeya's anger had changed to laughter
when she spoke of the clay fight he had with her friend Okawa. He
brought her a gift of sweet black berries and the tension between
them disappeared as soon as they shared them and talked more.

Tamataunee visited several more times after that. Often they
sat around the cooking fire inside and he told stories that had
been handed down for generations from elder to child. Sometimes
he and Ahmeya walked down to the lake, sat on the rocks, and
watched birds soar and dip over the water, catching bugs hovering
over the surface. Sometimes they walked in the woods along the
stream where they had met. Tamataunee taught Ahmeya what he
knew about the birds and animals of the forest. She learned how to
read the tracks of the animals and saw where they slept, flattened
grasses, and fed. Ahmeya taught Tamataunee more of the herbs
and plants growing in the woods around them. She would pluck
off a leaf and tell him "taste this," but sometimes it was a trick
and he would chew on something sour and unpleasant. Then he
would chase her and tell her she had to taste it too. They talked
of hopes for their lives and learned of each other's past. Ahmeya's
memories had faded with the years and when she spoke of her life

106

as a pioneer girl, she felt as if she were talking of someone else. Tamataunee was not bothered by her past, or the fact that she was really a white. He had lived by the lake all his life and had not been affected as much by the settlers' conflicts with the Indians as Ahmeya had. They shared their secrets and laughed at foolish things they had done. Both had great respect for the nature around them and were aware of the special gifts of the wild country they lived in and their Indian families. They grew closer to each other every day; so much that parting was becoming increasingly difficult for them.

After talking it over with Ahmeya, Tamataunee decided to offer Mahonoy a gift of wampum and furs in exchange for Ahmeya as his bride. When he approached Mahonoy about it, she was overjoyed, of course. She would not lose Ahmeya. When a daughter married in the Lenape village, she stayed in her mother's longhouse with her new husband. Mahonoy was gaining a son, one whom she already loved dearly, so gifts were cheerfully accepted and a ceremonial feast was prepared. Many Seneca and Lenape guests attended and watched a glowing, beautiful Ahmeya in a magnificent Indian wedding dress decorated with silver coins, colorful beads, and porcupine quills become a wife. Tamataunee was regal in his full Indian ceremonial attire. He and Ahmeya were married in a simple Indian ceremony where they declared to each other, "Kwichewël" which meant, "I marry you . . . I go with you." Mahonoy cried of course, even though she knew she'd soon see them both again. The singing and dancing of the wedding celebration went on late into the evening.

Ahmeya and Tamataunee decided after the feast to sneak off by themselves for a few days into the woods and camp by the stream where they first met. Tamataunee had built a comfortable lean-to there. Inside he laid a beautiful woven blanket and warm furs over a cushion of soft green moss. In front of the lean-to he built a campfire that gave them warmth and cast a golden light on their little shelter. That night they looked at the stars twinkling between the forest canopy and talked of being together forever. Ahmeya wanted to have children and raise them in the Indian ways. Among the scent of pine trees and to the music of the waterfall, Ahmeya became Tamataunee's wife. Tamataunee was patient and passionately tender with her. They sat together on the blanket and Ahmeya was initially afraid and trembled when he touched her. Her eyes were tearful with emotion. He held her face and lovingly kissed her forehead, her eyelids, and the nape of her neck. All the dreaming and passion they had been holding back was intensified with each touch of bare flesh or kiss of their lips. Soon there was no talking, only the intense passion between them. They were lost in each other and later slept peacefully, arms encircled, exhausted, and too happy to even dream that night. They stayed in the forest several days. They hiked to lookouts where they could view miles of valleys and forest vistas. They saw the big lake shimmering in the sunshine and becoming golden with the sunsets. They gathered wild food and just spent time alone together. Before long, they would have to return to the longhouse of Mahonoy. There they would have their own separate living area and start building their life together; but for this short time, it was just Ahmeya and Tamataunee alone in their own wild world.

After their return, Tamataunee quickly settled into his duties as a man of Mahonoy's longhouse and brought back fish and game from hunting trips. Ahmeya had been trained well by Mahonoy and prepared food at her own cooking fire although they often ate with Mahonoy. Sometimes they would visit her for a meal she cooked and when asked, she would join them at their fire. Ahmeya and Tamataunee settled comfortably into life at the happy longhouse of Mahonoy.

CHAPTER 15

*1779, Three years later at Ina and Cornelius's
cabin on the Pennsylvania frontier.*

I T HAD TAKEN MANY MONTHS FOR Ina's raw wounds to heal
after being kidnapped and then escaping from the Indians.
Now years later, she still limped terribly and had to use a cane.
She would always have physical and emotional scars from her
time in captivity. She looked like a woman much older than
she actually was. Her hair was prematurely gray and she kept
it pulled back tightly into a bun at the back of her head. Her
thin body bent like a birch tree after an ice storm. She always wore
dark colored clothes with high collars buttoned tight at her neck,
long sleeves, and skirt hems all the way to the floor. She started
wearing mourning clothes after her return from capture, and it became her regular manner of dress.

Ina's days were filled with the chores of keeping a home. She
woke before dawn, got the snuffed-out candle at her bedside and
carried it in the dark to the kitchen area where she sat it on the
mantle over the fireplace. She would use it later when the sun re-
tired. Then Ina grabbed the metal fire poker, stirred together the
glowing coals of the dying fire and heaped some kindling on to get it
burning again and warm the chilly room. Before her day was over,
Ina would have cooked breakfast for Cornelius and Christopher, fed
the dogs, gathered the eggs, emptied the chamber pot, weeded in
the garden, picked vegetables, made remedies for sickness, washed
and hung clothes, baked bread, killed and dressed a chicken for

the evening meal, made candles and swept away dirt and cobwebs. After cleaning up from dinner, she spent her evenings sitting by the fire altering or sewing clothes for others with her mother's precious thimble protecting her finger.

She kept their cabin as clean as it could possibly be and worked constantly all day at some chore so that when she lay down at night her body and mind would be too exhausted for any possibility of nightmares. But at times, she would think and wonder, *Was Amelia still out there in the Indian country? If she were here with us now, she would be married, and I would have grandchildren to hold and sew for. If he had lived, Rubin would be here to help Cornelius with his work, and we could be a family again instead of this emptiness I feel.* Though she was very grateful she had Cornelius and Christopher, her recurring memories and thoughts of her lost children would send her into a deep depression that would last for days from the weight of it.

Her wounded heart and mind were deeply altered and ulcerated with bitterness. She had lost her son and didn't know if her daughter was still alive, and if she was, she must surely be living with those horrible savages. That was something she had never gotten over or could forgive the Indians for. She passed her loathing of the savages on to her single surviving child, Christopher, at every chance. He was the baby she had carried out of the woods and saved from the barbarians. She constantly reminded him of that experience and their close call with slavery and death. She never went into the woods to gather hickory nuts again, nor did she ever go far from the cabin for any reason. She was too frightened by all the things she now knew were lurking in the woods.

Every night the doors were all securely bolted, a loaded gun made ready, and she checked and rechecked to make sure doors and window shutters were locked up tight. Even if she was exhausted, sometimes when she finally closed her eyes, nightmares of the Indians breaking in returned. She often woke in a cold sweat and reached for Cornelius. It was impossible for Cornelius to leave her alone to go hunting. She insisted Christopher stay behind with her or they had to take her to stay with a neighbor. Cornelius had gotten her a pair of big, loud dogs who barked in alarm at any strange noise to make her feel safer. They had closer neighbors now, but Ina still felt insecure and afraid all the time. Cornelius was often impatient with her excessive fears. She was still a good wife to him and took good care of the cabin and their son, but her mind had been so altered by the trauma of the kidnapping that she was never quite the same and had difficulty finding happiness in anything. Her inability to put the tragedy behind her made them all unhappy and miserable. Ina would read her Bible and often loudly quoted scripture to them about an eye for an eye justice. Many times, she clutched a large handmade wooden cross that hung by a leather thong around her neck and muttered to herself.

Cornelius had also been tormented by the loss of his two children. He too had developed strong negative feelings about all Indians. He was especially angry about what had happened to his wife's mind. Cornelius felt they had taken the woman he had married from him and left him with an embittered cripple in her place. Ina was such an unhappy woman, haunted by demons and memories of the past that still lived with her every day.

Cornelius never missed a chance to help drive Indians out of the territory or punish any "peaceful Indians" that were caught violating the laws of the Commonwealth. There were several converted Indians at the Moravian Mission not far away. Cornelius trusted none of them.

"They only want free board and vittles and are too lazy to work fer 'em. Once a savage, always a savage," he testified many times. He thought it was like trying to tame a wolf, "You can't nivver trust 'em, they'll turn on ya evry time!"

Christopher was fifteen years old and had no recollection of being taken by the Indians, but he'd heard of the kidnapping of his mother and the murder of his brother repeatedly over the years. He knew he had a sister Amelia who may be alive somewhere in the wilderness, or perhaps she was dead by now, no one really knew. They and others had tried to find her, but never had any luck. The years of teaching had made him an Indian hater too. Just like his father, he was eager to use his gun and knife against them.

Cornelius had built a small sawmill on Sugar Creek right near his cabin. So much of the forest had been cleared away over the years that Ina could see the roof of the mill from her cabin window, which made her feel safer. Cornelius would come back during the day to check on her too. His mill was busy with settlers bringing wagon loads of logs to saw into boards. The plentiful white pine was being cut down and used locally as well as being floated down large creeks and rivers as rafts to cities far below them.

There was a great demand for sawed lumber now for homes instead of just building with logs. Barns and other buildings were easier to construct and other uses for the sawed boards such as plank floors and furniture were desired by the more sophisticated settlers, so Cornelius and Christopher were kept busy working close to Ina and filling orders every day. Occasionally Christopher could get away for a short while to hunt with a friend. He was such a good marksman with his Pennsylvania long rifle, he seldom missed any game and wasn't gone for long.

Men coming to the sawmill often told Cornelius and Christopher about settlers working fields not far away who had been clubbed or shot and scalped, and several hunters that were ambushed in the woods by Indians. Search parties had found them later brutalized and murdered. Cows and horses were being slaughtered in pastures and there were reports of whole families disappearing and nothing left of their homesteads except a burned-out cabin and dead livestock. Some homesteaders on the frontier were so afraid of a hostile Indian raid they were giving up and returning to live closer to the small towns now populating the area.

Lately, there had been several Indian raids throughout the territory. Many of the raids were close to Ina and Cornelius' settlement and everyone was uneasy and anxious. They were sick of the constant threat of uprisings and the fear of being attacked. Cornelius and Christopher kept their guns handy for quick use if needed. "Let 'em move out ter the west by the Ohio Country," Cornelius kept saying. "There's plenty of land out thet way and we'll all be a might better when they git gone! Either that or burn 'em all out." Ina was more frightened than usual and kept a sharp butcher knife under her feather pillow. She often shook Cornelius awake at night because she heard a strange noise. It was always just a tree branch scratching the wall, or the wind moving a shutter, but Cornelius had to get up and check every noise out before she would let him lie down and go back to sleep. Then, if the dogs barked at an owl hooting or any other noise, he had to get up again to investigate.

One week, bad news was swiftly traveling through the settlement from cabin to cabin. More vicious raids by the Indians had taken place. The Commonwealth authorities and the leaders in Washington agreed this hostile Indian problem had gone on far too long already. The authorities wanted the settlers to feel safe so more would keep moving into the new territories and needed them to get their claims established for the strength of the Colonies. Otherwise, the French or Dutch might try to move their people in and take over vast blocks of land. George Washington decided after he heard of the new Indian raids and deaths of the settlers to send General Sullivan north. He would travel to northern Pennsylvania, up the Susquehanna River, and purge the area all-around of Indians. He would have a force of over four thousand men to clear all the savages out. Sullivan's orders from General Washington were that the immediate object is the total destruction and devastation of the Indian settlements. It was essential to ruin their crops and prevent them from planting more. And, do not by any means listen to any overture of peace before total ruinment of their settlements is done.

The campaign started in early Summer of 1779. The soldiers followed the Indian trail known as the Great Warrior Path northward along the banks of the Susquehanna River. Cannons and supplies were sent upstream by barges rowed by soldiers. When night fell, the barges would pull into shore and the marching soldiers and officers on horses camped nearby along the banks of the Susquehanna.

Sullivan's forces reached settlements on their march north some miles below the confluence of two rivers. Most of the Indians had already been pushed out of there and settlers had moved onto the fertile river bottom lands. The cabin of Cornelius and Ina with their son Christopher, now a teenager, was located there. When the homesteaders along the route of the march saw all the troops coming through, they met them by foot and on horses. They raised their muskets and rifles and cheered them on. Many of the men, young and old, asked to join in as volunteers to help rout the Indians, and General Sullivan gladly accepted their offer. Ina pleaded with Cornelius and Christopher to go and kill some of the savages just for her.

She said, "If you won't do it fer me, do it for Rubin and Amelia." Ina wanted to go herself and said she would "enjoy sinkin' a butcher knife into them Indians hearts," but knew she couldn't travel in her physical condition. She'd stay with a neighbor close by for safety while Cornelius and Christopher were gone.

The troops pushed further north past the former Indian castle called Queen Esther's Flats to the junction of the Chemung and Susquehanna Rivers to a spot the Indians called Teaoga. The rivers were at their lowest this time of the year so it was possible to manage crossings in places. Here they burned every longhouse they found and killed any Indians who hadn't fled into woods already. Late that night some of the settlers that had joined the soldiers along the way talked of the Indians who lived in this area among the white settlers. Some men spoke against the converted Indians who lived at a Moravian Mission not far away. They were sure the Indians were sneaking out after dark and taking part in the raids that were happening. Drunken men got each other stirred up and agitated. The more they drank and talked, the crazier they became. Some of them rode out to the Moravian mission with hatred in their hearts and liquor surging hot in their veins. They broke in on the peaceful Indians who had no warning that anything was wrong. The Christian Indians, confused and not understanding what was happening, didn't even run away at first. Then, when they realized the men were attacking them, they tried to escape, but it was too late. They were trapped and the drunken settlers and soldiers killed every Indian man, woman, and child in the Mission that night. Then the party, satiated by the gore, rode back north to rejoin Sullivan's forces and brag loudly about their victory.

Sullivan had camped with his army at Teaoga to plan and prepare for the attack on the Seneca country to the northwest. After resting for a few days and getting supplies, the soldiers regained their strength and resumed the fateful march northward. The air was full of excitement on the drive. Their newly formed country, religion, and beliefs all supported this cause. This was justice for all the Indians had done to the settlers. God wanted them to live in these lands. These Indians were savages, not men who worshipped the true God, they all agreed. The men fed each other's frenzy to get rid of the Indians once and for all as they marched. General Washington had given specific orders to lay waste to everything in Indian country and they were eager to fulfill his command. Some had also heard of the bounty the Commonwealth of Pennsylvania was paying for Indian prisoners and scalps and wanted to make some money. They were offering a reward of three thousand dollars for every Indian prisoner or Tory acting with them and a reward of two thousand and five hundred dollars for every Indian scalp. It was to be paid in Continental dollars. That was worth thirty-three dollars in silver and made many soldiers eager to cash in on the offer and kill an Indian. Whenever they stopped, they sharpened their knives, checked their gunpowder, and made sure their guns were primed and ready for action.

Cornelius and Christopher rode right along with the soldiers and other volunteers that had horses. They all talked of the honor of warfare and the challenge of hand-to-hand combat. Cornelius told them of his wife's ordeal with the Lenape years before. Many of the militia volunteers had suffered personal tragedies by Indians also and were eager to engage them in combat.

CHAPTER 16

THE COMBINED CONTINENTAL FORCES WITH General Sullivan in command and General Clinton as his second numbered over four thousand when they set off from Teaoga. They had cleared all the Indians from that fertile valley area where the Chemung and west branch of the Susquehanna Rivers met. Longhouses had been burned, natives killed or taken as prisoners, and the settlers there felt they finally had help with the Indian problem. Now it was necessary to strike deep into the interior of the Indian country. The weather had been extremely hot even for August. General Sullivan warned his men to fill their canteens and march forward at a deliberate pace, but to conserve energy for any impending battles. The men and horses were all getting overheated marching in the strong sun, but if they rested too often, the Indians in their camps would surely be forewarned of their approach and escape before they reached them. As they travelled northward, they came across more Indian homes. Each one was quickly burned, its inhabitants killed, and all left behind as flames and ashes.

Dust clouds rose from the tramping of the boots, hooves, and wagon wheels. The orders were to be as quiet as possible as they marched forward. "Keep on the lookout for hostiles in the woods you are travelling through," they were told. "And stop any you see from escaping and warning the others." A surprise attack on the Indians' villages would yield the most destruction and casualties.

Sullivan was worried about the rising from dust from such a large army being noticed from a distance, but a quick rain went over that dampened the soil and refreshed the excited but weary soldiers. The Oneida Indian scouts had returned and told Sullivan there was a large encampment a short march away by Seneca lake. The order was given to stop and rest just a couple miles before the place where Mahonoy and the other Lenape had their longhouses. While stopped, the men checked their guns, adjusted their flint and powder, and made sure their bayonets were secured for battle.

Sullivan rode through the ranks of men who were leaning on artillery wagons, resting against trees, or sitting down quietly, giving them encouragement and orders to spare none. A young flag bearer waving the new American flag with thirteen stars rode beside him.

Then he stopped his horse near a group and the soldiers stood up and gathered around him to listen. Cornelius and Christopher were among them and moved closer to hear the voice of their commander.

"These hostile Indians need to be reprimanded in the harshest way possible so their atrocities against the citizens will stop forever." General Sullivan said. "You brave men are doing this for God and your new country." He told them. "You will make families safe on the frontier and rid this land of godless barbarians who will kill you, your wife, and your children and take your scalps if they have a chance. They not only war against us, they aid our enemies, the British. Take any food and provisions you find for ourselves and then destroy their gardens and orchards. If we don't kill them in combat, we will kill them with famine. We must show them that we are stronger and more powerful and there are many, many more of us than them so they do not dare challenge our authority and ownership of this country any longer," he continued. "This is our land now! Show no mercy men!" He concluded as he turned back and rode to the head of the line. Shortly after the order was given to move forward at a more rapid pace and after marching for a little more than an hour, the villages of the Lenape and Seneca were just over the hill.

The Indians were busy that day. The corn was ripe in the field and women and children were filling baskets with ears and carrying them to the longhouses. The squash vines and beans were wilting in the dryness of late summer and some were carrying water from a stream to them. Older children were busy on raised wooden platforms in the corn field spinning a leather thong with a rock tied to the end of it over their heads. It made a humming noise while they loudly shouted to scare the crows and ravens away from the ripening corn. Indian men were on the shore of the lake unloading baskets of fish that they had netted earlier from their canoes. Others having most of their outdoor work done, or who were old or weak, had sought shelter from the hot sun inside the welcoming shade of their longhouses. The oldest Indians were inside with children husking the corn, tying the ears together, and hanging them from the rafters. Others were still out in the orchards picking the remainder of the peaches and cherries or looking for early apples.

Sullivan had been worried that the Indians might have been warned of their coming, but he needn't be. Not one Indian had escaped to run northward and warn the others. The Indians never imagined American troops would invade the heart of the Iroquois Confederacy, the powerful alliance of six Haudenosaunee nations. They felt safe that August day working in the sunshine by the sparkling lake and readying provisions for the coming winter. It was a surprise to Mahonoy and the people of her longhouse when so many armed troops came pouring over the hill and trapped them in their village tucked back along the edge of the forest. It didn't matter whether they were Indian men, women, or children. None were spared from the frenzy of the men filled with hate and murderous intentions against a culture they didn't understand. It was revenge they were after, "an eye for an eye." It was a righteous cause in the minds of the entire horde that was attacking that day.

The Indians were killed by gunshot, sabers, knives, or clubbing with rifle butts. The soldiers used any ghastly means they could to destroy. It was war at its cruelest. Some victims even burned to death, lying wounded in the searing heat of the flaming wood and bark longhouses. Some were trampled by charging horses as soldiers chased them down. Fields of ripening crops were set ablaze and exploded into tall orange walls of fire in the dry heat of the August day. Any cattle or animals were slaughtered in the riot and glut of the massacre. The sky was black with huge billowing plumes of smoke and the air was heavy with the acrid smell of burning longhouses and flesh. Soldiers cut belts of bark all around the trunks of apple, peach and cherry trees that had been cultivated for generations so they would die too. When they were finished, not even a hand-woven basket had escaped conversion to smoldering black ashes. Everything was "laid to waste," as General Washington had commanded, and the soldiers felt the mission of their surprise attack was a success. They whooped, hollered, and danced around, congratulating each other among the slaughtered bodies of Indians. Generations of wisdom and heritage died that day on Seneca Lake.

Ahmeya had left the longhouse early in the morning carrying her little daughter, Kuskusky, with her. Mahonoy had not been feeling well and Ahmeya wanted to gather some herbs to brew a healing tea for her. She walked high up into the deep woods that rose above the village to collect plants. Kuskusky sat playing among the soft green ferns while Ahmeya dug roots and gathered leaves. When Ahmeya heard the first muffled sounds of gunfire, she was initially puzzled, and then alarmed. She stood there and listened intently for several moments trying to decipher what she had heard and the direction it was coming from. It couldn't be hunters, she thought, there were too many guns going off at the same time. Then she heard the faint distant screams of the Indians, young and old, and the shouts of the men attacking. She dropped the basket of herbs, scooped up her daughter, and started running towards the longhouses of her people.

She could hardly breathe, fright was choking her so. It felt as if she were trying to painfully swallow a chunk of food that was much too large. It took her breath away and brought tears to her eyes. Her village was being attacked, but by who? Was it a warring party of their enemies, the Mohawks? Mahonoy, Tamataunee, and her other relatives and friends were all back at the longhouses. She ran as fast as she could and the closer she got, the worse it sounded. She almost tripped and fell. Her feet pounded the ground as she dodged roots and rocks in her way. She pushed back limbs with her hands as she bolted through the woods holding tightly onto her daughter. She came to just within the edge of the trees that overlooked the place where the longhouses were.

There, through the smoke and flames, she saw the soldiers advancing and her Lenape friends trying to escape. Some were valiantly trying to defend their longhouses. Others, in sheer terror, were trying to flee into the woods. She stood rooted to that spot and looked down at the atrocious sight of the Indian men, women, and children being chased down and run through with bayonets. Soldiers on horses clubbed their heads with rifle butts. Many fell forward onto their knees, prayer like, and then dove forward again, face smashing into the dirt. Several Indians were courageously trying to fight, but they were greatly outnumbered.

Ahmeya saw an Indian woman run screaming, arms beating the air, hair and clothes all afire, the men laughing at her horrific movements. The soldiers hooted and hollered at the sight as if it were entertainment. Ahmeya's tear-filled eyes blurred her vision as she searched for the people of her longhouse. Off to the side by the stream where they washed clothes, she saw an old woman crouching down and Tamataunee, her brave husband, standing over her. A horse rider charged at them both, swinging his saber in the air above his head. Ahmeya watched in horror, hugging her baby as the rider sliced at Tamataunee. He managed to duck the saber and raised his tomahawk to fight back, but before he could strike a blow at his attacker, another man using a long rifle shot Tamataunee. He fell to his knees, looked up at the saber-carrying horseman, who then kicked him in the head. It snapped backwards, and he fell to the ground with a thud.

Ahmeya looked away, unable yet to process what she just saw. To her left, she could now see a familiar woman cowering before an armed rider. The old woman raised her arms, pleading, and was quickly shot by the same soldier with the long rifle. The men then turned and faced the burning longhouses, lifting their arms in victory over their enemy. Ahmeya got a good look at their war-crazed faces. The younger man was just a teenager, a stranger to her. Then a deep, mournful sound escaped her lips when she saw the face of the other man. He was older, gray haired and thinner than she had remembered, but she was sure it was her father, Cornelius.

The sounds of the battle and carnage muffled the scream that came from the depths of Ahmeya's soul. Her whole life was lying in front of her. The people she loved most deeply were dead. Her home and village were burning to ashes before her eyes. Her love, Tamataunee, whose arms had made her feel so safe and secure, was gone. To look into his loving eyes had made her feel as if she were touching his soul. Her gentle Lenape mother, Mahonoy, had taught her patience and kindness and all the ways of the wild things that she loved. They were lying there where they had fallen in the dirt beside each other.

They were both dead now, she was sure of it, and she had seen her father, who she had remembered as a hardworking, honest man she had laughed and played games of checkers with as a child, take part in the massacre. To see him now, this monster, this demon that had taken her happiness away, chilled her. No, much more than that, it repulsed her, and she realized she no longer considered him her father. She stayed riveted to that spot, hidden just behind some pine trees. Blinding tears streamed down her face. She shuddered violently with the shock of it all and was racked with overwhelming grief. Then Kuskusky stirred and she forced herself to breathe deeply. She slowed down her racing thoughts and tried to clear her head. She couldn't watch any longer. The troops were taking scalps, congratulating each other and robbing the Indian bodies of beads and wish tokens. She became afraid now for her daughter; she had to save her baby. Kuskusky was all she had left of her love with Tamataunee and her life with Mahonoy and the Lenape.

Ahmeya decided to leave that place right then and start walking west, where the sun rested. She would try to find some other Indian allies there. She would have to make a big loop around to the north, staying far above the now burned out Seneca village. She would have to walk all the way around the top of the big lake, staying in the woods to avoid the soldiers. She could do it; she knew how to survive in the woods. And she was strong, young, and Lenape. She needed to get away from there now.

"I will raise you Lenape, my little child," she said to her baby as she turned away from the massacre, the sounds of the soldiers, and the all-consuming flames. "And I will teach you the ways of the Seneca too," she told her, looking into Kuskusky's dark eyes and kissing her small head. "I will tell you of the stories of the generations," she whispered, taking another determined step northward. "And of your wise grandmother, Mahonoy, head of a sacred longhouse of many Lenape Indians. I will tell you of the Little People of the Woods, who help us, and of your father Tamataunee, a proud and mighty Seneca brave of the Turtle Clan." She walked further away into the deep blue shadows of the Eastern pine forest and continued. "I will tell you of the Great Spirit Nanapush who climbed a tree and saved the animals from a flood. I will tell you of turtle and how earth came to be," she said as she walked on. "I will tell you of the healing plants of the woods and the spirits of the trees and rocks and animals that are our brothers and sisters," she said as she disappeared into the depths of the tender ferns and the ancient listening trees. The sound of her voice drifted slowly back on the breath of the wind. "I will tell you Kuskusky. . . . I will tell you."

THE END

ABOUT THE AUTHOR

DORIS WILBUR is an author who lives in rural New York State and writes historical fiction. Her stories are infused with nature and the outdoors as her characters face challenges in their lives and choices they must make to be successful.

Doris spent much of her career as a commercial artist and award winning watercolor artist. She was a public-school art teacher also, but behind the scenes, she always wrote. She has worked for newspapers, advertising agencies, school systems, and had a graphic design business.

She and her husband Jerry raised five children and have lived in New York State, Pennsylvania, Maryland, and Florida. She has worked in the large cities of Washington, DC; Orlando, Florida; and Syracuse, NY, as well as living the rural life.

She graduated summa cum laude from Mansfield University of Pennsylvania where she studied Creative Writing, Botany, and Art Education. Now, she and her husband live at a private lake surrounded by woods and nature where she continues to teach and write.

Made in the USA
Lexington, KY
25 September 2018